MW00980425

BRIAN LUMLEY

BOB EGGLETON

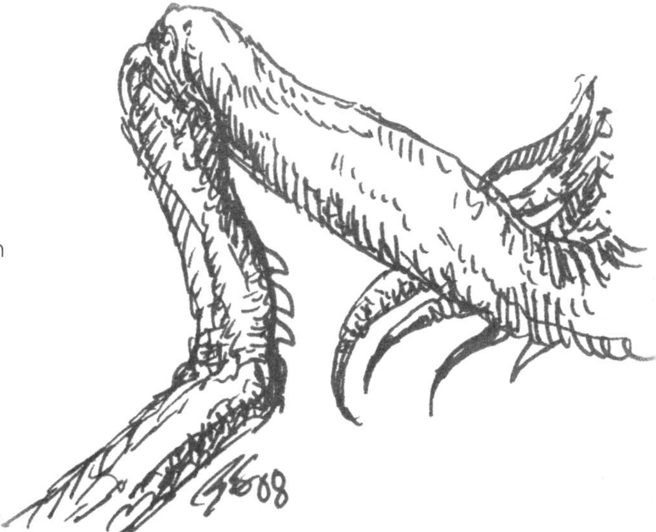

This special

signed edition

is limited to

1500 copies.

THE

NONESUCH

AND OTHERS

THE

NONESUCH

AND OTHERS

BRIAN LUMLEY

SUBTERRANEAN PRESS 2009

First Edition

ISBN
978-1-59606-210-8

Subterranean Press
PO Box 190106
Burton, MI 48519

www.subterraneanpress.com

Table of Contents:

INTRODUCTION

THE MAN WHO FEATURES in the following trilogy of stories is in no way typical of a majority of characters in my other stories and novels, for by and large I write of heroes. And the reason I make no mention of his name is because—like Clint Eastwood in those spaghetti westerns—he doesn't have a name; I didn't give him one. And even when he gives *himself* one in this small book's title story, it's a pseudonym.

You'll see what I mean.

*Un*like that cheroot-smoking fellow in the poncho, however, and as I've hinted above, *my* Man With No Name isn't a hero nor even an anti-hero. (But he's no coward either, well not especially.) Why, in *The Nonesuch* he might even appear rather brave—or perhaps stupid and ridiculously naive, depending on your point of view.

But however you look at it, my Man With No Name is just an innocent bystander who happens to be standing by in the wrong place at the wrong time: a witness to terrifying occurrences, monstrous events, who can never be one hundred per cent positive that the things he has experienced are real. And why not? Because a man who sees pink elephants might as easily see just about anything!

So then, and as stated, this rather different character of mine is by no means a typical hero; but if *you* the reader were confronted by the bizarre, inexplicable nonesuches whose paths tend to cross his in the following stories...well, how brave would you be?

Ask yourself that question when you're done...

Brian Lumley
Devon, Feb. 2008

The Thin People

The Thin People

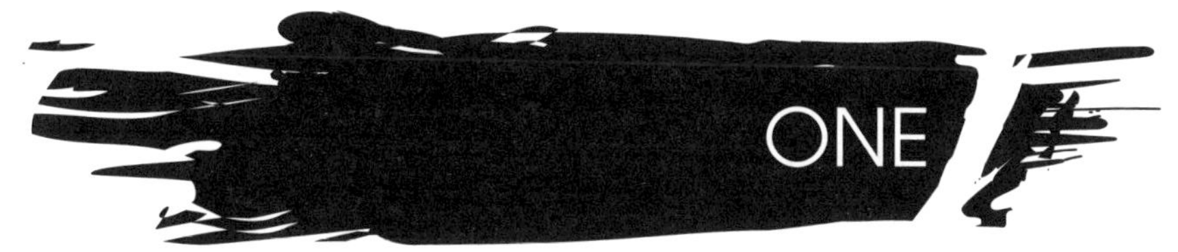

ONE

Sunny place, Barrows Hill. Not *Barrow's* Hill, no. Barrows without the apostrophe. For instance: you won't find it on any map. You'll find maps whose borders approach it, whose corners impinge, however slightly, upon it, but in general it seems that cartographers avoid it. It's too far out from the centre for the tubes, hasn't got a mainline station, has lost much of its integrity by virtue of all the infernal demolition and reconstruction going on around and within it. But it's still there. Buses run to and from, and the older folk who live there still call it Barrows Hill.

When I went to live there in the late seventies I hated the place. There was a sense of senility, of inherent idiocy about it. A damp sort of place. Even under a hot summer sun, damp. You could feel blisters of fungus rising even under the freshest paint. Not that the place got painted very much. Not that I saw, anyway. No, for it was like somewhere out of Lovecraft: decaying, diseased, inbred.

Barrows Hill. I didn't stay long, a few months. Too long, really. It gave you the feeling that if you delayed, if you stood still for just one extra moment, then it would grow up over you and you'd become a part of it. There are some old, old places in London, and I reckoned Barrows Hill was one of the oldest. I also reckoned it for its *genius loci*; like it was a focal point for secret things. Or perhaps not a focal point, for that might suggest a radiation—a spreading outwards—and as I've said Barrows Hill was ingrown. The last bastion of the strange old things of London. Things like the thin people. The very tall, very thin people.

Now nobody—but nobody *anywhere*—is ever going to believe me about the thin people, which is one of the two reasons I'm not afraid to tell this story. The other is that I don't live there any more. But when I did…

I suspect now that quite a few people—ordinary people, that is—knew about them. They wouldn't admit it, that's all, and probably still won't. And since all of the ones who'd know live on Barrows Hill, I really can't say I blame 'em. There was one old lad lived there, however, who knew *and* talked about them. To me. Since he had a bit of a reputation (to be frank, they called him 'Barmy Bill of Barrows Hill') I didn't pay a deal of attention at first. I mean, who would?

Barrows Hill had a pub, a couple of pubs, but the one most frequented was The Railway. A hangover from a time when there really was a railway, I supposed. A couple of years ago there had been another, a serious rival to The Railway for a little while, when someone converted an old block into a fairly modem pub. But it didn't last. Whoever owned the place might have known something, but probably not. Or he wouldn't have been so stupid as to call his place The Thin Man! It was only open for a week or two before burning down to the ground.

But that was before my time and the only reason I make mention of pubs, and particularly The Railway, is because that's where I met Barmy Bill. He was there because of his disease, alcoholism, and I was there because of mine, heartsickness—which, running at a high fever, showed all signs of mutating pretty soon into Bill's problem. In short, I was hitting the bottle.

Now this is all incidental information, of course, and I don't intend to go into it other than to say it was our problems brought us together. As unlikely a friendship as any you might imagine. But Barmy Bill was good at listening, and I was good at buying booze. And so we were good company.

One night, however, when I ran out of money, I made the mistake of inviting him back to my place. (My place—hah! A bed, a loo and a typewriter; a poky little place up some wooden stairs, like a penthouse kennel; oh, yes, and a bonus in the shape of a cupboard converted to a shower.) But I had a couple bottles of beer back there and a half-bottle of gin, and when I'd finished crying on Barmy Bill's shoulder it wouldn't be far for me to fall into bed. What did surprise me was how hard it was to get him back there. He started complaining the moment we left the bar—or rather, as soon as he saw which way we were headed.

"Up the Larches? You live up there off Barchington Road? Yes, I remember you told me. Well, and maybe I'll just stay in the pub a while after all. I mean, if you live right up *there*—well, it's out of my way, isn't it?"

"Out of your way? It's a ten-minute walk, that's all! I thought you were thirsty?"

"Thirsty I am—always! Barmy I'm not—they only say I am 'cos they're frightened to listen to me."

"They?"

"People!" he snapped, sounding unaccustomedly sober. Then, as if to change the subject: "A half-bottle of gin, you said?"

'That's right, Gordon's. But if you want to get back on down to The Railway…"

"No, no, we're half-way there now," he grumbled, hurrying along beside me, almost taking my arm in his nervousness. "And anyway, it's a nice bright night tonight. They're not much for light nights."

"They?" I asked again.

"People!" Despite his short, bowed legs, he was half a pace ahead of me. "The thin people." But where his first word had been a snarl, his last three were whispered, so that I almost missed them entirely.

Then we were up Larches Avenue—*the* Larches as Barmy Bill had it—and closing fast on 22, and suddenly it was very quiet. Only the scrape of dry, blown leaves on the pavement. Autumn, and the trees half-naked. Moonlight falling through webs of high, black, brittle branches.

"Plenty of moon," said Bill, his voice hushed. "Thank God—in whom I really don't believe—for that. *But no street lights*! You see that? Bulbs all missing. That's them."

"Them?" I caught his elbow, turning him into my gateway—if there'd been a gate. There wasn't, just the post, which served as my landmark whenever I'd had a skinful.

"Them, yes!" he snapped, staring at me as I turned my key in the lock. "Damn young fool!"

And so up the creaky stairs to my little cave of solitude, and Barmy Bill shivering despite the closeness of the night and warmth of the place, which leeched a lot of its heat from the houses on both sides, and from the flat below, whose elderly lady occupier couldn't seem to live in anything other than an oven; and in through my own door, into the 'living' room, where Bill closed the curtains across the jutting bay windows as if he'd lived there all of his life. But not before he'd peered out into the night street, his eyes darting this way and that, round and bright in his lined, booze-desiccated face.

Barmy, yes. Well, maybe he was and maybe he wasn't. "Gin," I said, passing him the bottle and a glass. "But go easy, yes? I like a nip myself, you know."

"A nip? A nip? Huh! If I lived here I'd need more than a nip. This is the middle of it, this is. The very middle!"

"Oh?" I grinned. "Myself, I had it figured for the living end!"

He paced the floor for a few moments—three paces there, three back—across the protesting boards of my tiny room, before pointing an almost accusing finger at me. "Chirpy tonight, aren't you? Full of beans!"

"You think so?" Yes, he was right. I did feel a bit brighter. "Maybe I'm over it, eh?"

He sat down beside me. "I certainly hope so, you daft young sod! And now maybe you'll pay some attention to my warnings and get yourself a place well away from here."

"Your warnings? Have you been warning me, then?" It dawned on me that he had, for several weeks, but I'd been too wrapped up in my own misery to pay him much heed. And who would? After all, he was Barmy Bill.

"Course I have!" he snapped. "About them bloody—"

"Thin people," I finished it for him. "Yes, I remember now."

"Well?"

"Eh?"

"Are you or aren't you?"

"I'm listening, yes."

"No, no, *no*! Are you or aren't you going to find yourself new lodgings?"

"When I can afford it, yes."

"You're in danger here, you know? They don't like strangers. Strangers change things, and they're against that. They don't like anything strange, nothing new. They're a dying breed, I fancy, but while they're here they'll keep things the way they like 'em."

"OK," I sighed. "This time I really am listening. You want to start at the beginning?"

He answered my sigh with one of his own, shook his head impatiently. "Daft young bugger! If I didn't like you I wouldn't bother. But all right, for your own good, one last time…just listen and I'll tell you what I know. It's not much, but it's the last warning you'll get…"

BEST THING EVER HAPPENED for 'em must have been the lampposts, I reckon."

"Dogs?" I raised my eyebrows.

He glared at me and jumped to his feet. "Right, that's it. I'm off."

"Oh, sit down, sit down!' I calmed him. "Here, fill your glass again. And I promise I'll try not to interrupt."

"Lampposts!" he snapped, his brows black as thunder. But he sat and took the drink. "Yes, for they imitate 'em, see? And thin, they can hide behind 'em. Why, they can stand so still that on a dark night you wouldn't know the difference! Can you imagine that, eh? Hiding behind or imitating a lamppost!"

I tried to imagine it, but: "Not really," I had to admit. Now, however, my levity was becoming a bit forced. There was something about his intensity—the way his limbs shook in a manner other than alcoholic—which was getting through to me. "Why should they hide?"

"Freaks! Wouldn't you hide? A handful of them. Millions of us. We'd hound 'em out, kill 'em off!"

"So why don't we?"

"'Cos we're all smart young buggers like you, that's why! 'Cos we don't *believe* in 'em."

"But you do?"

Bill nodded, his three- or four-day growth of hair quivering on jowls and upper lip. "Seen 'em," he said, "and seen…*evidence* of them."

"And they're real people? I mean, you know, human? Just like me and you, except…thin?"

"And tall. Oh—*tall*!"

"Tall?" I frowned. "Thin and tall. How tall? Not as tall as—"

"Lampposts," he nodded, "yes. Not during the day, mind you, only at night. At night they—" (he looked uncomfortable, as if it had suddenly dawned on him how crazy this all must sound) "—they sort of, well, kind of *unfold* themselves."

I thought about it, nodded. "They unfold themselves. Yes, I see."

"No, you don't see," his voice was flat, cold, angry now. "But you will, if you hang around here long enough."

"Where do they live," I asked, "these tall, thin people?"

"In thin houses," he answered, matter-of-factly.

"Thin houses?"

"Sure! Are you telling me you haven't noticed the thin houses? Why, this place of yours very nearly qualifies! Thin houses, yes. Places where normal people wouldn't dream of setting up. There's half-a-dozen such in Barchington, and a couple right here in the Larches!" He shuddered and I bent to turn on an extra bar in my electric fire.

"Not cold, mate," Bill told me then. "Hell no! Enough booze in me to keep me warm. But I shudder every time I think of 'em. I mean, what *do* they do?"

"Where do they work, you mean?"

"Work?" he shook his head. "No, they don't work. Probably do a bit of tealeafing. Burglary, you know. Oh, they'd get in anywhere, the thin people. But what do they *do*?"

I shrugged.

"I mean, me and you, we watch telly, play cards, chase the birds, read the paper. But them…?"

It was on the tip of my tongue to suggest maybe they go into the woods and frighten owls, but suddenly I didn't feel half so flippant. "You said you'd seen them?"

"Seen 'em sure enough, once or twice," he confirmed. "And weird! One, I remember, came out of his thin house in Barchington; I could show you it some time in daylight. Me, I was behind a hedge sleeping it off. Don't ask me how I got there, drunk as a lord! Anyway, something woke me up.

"Down at its bottom the hedge was thin where cats come through. It was night and the council men had been round during the day putting bulbs in the street lights, so the place was all lit up. And directly opposite, there's this thin house and its door slowly opening; and out comes this bloke into the night, half of him yellow from the lamplight and half black in shadow. See, right there in front of the thin house is a street lamp.

"But this chap looks normal enough, you know? A bit stiff in his movements; he sort of moves jerky, like them contortionists who hook their feet over their shoulders and walk on their hands. Anyway, he looks up and down the street, and he's obviously satisfied no one's there. Then…

"He slips back a little into the shadows until he comes up against the wall of his house, and he—unfolds!

"I see the light glinting down one edge of him, see it suddenly split into two edges at the bottom, sort of hinged at the top. And the split widens until he stands in the dark there like a big pair of dividers. And then one half swings up until it forms a straight line, perpendicular—and now he's ten feet tall. Then the same again, only this time the division takes place in the middle. Like…like a joiner's wooden three-foot ruler, with hinges so he can open it up, you know?"

I nodded, fascinated despite myself. "And that's how they're built, eh? I mean, well, hinged?"

"Hell, no!" he snorted. "You can fold your arms on your elbows, can't you? Or your legs on your knees? You can bend from the waist and touch your toes? Well I sure can! Their joints may be a little different from ours, that's all—maybe like the joints of certain insects. Or maybe not. I mean, their science is different from ours, too. Perhaps they fold and unfold themselves the same way they do it to other things—except it doesn't do them any harm. I dunno…"

"What?" I asked, puzzled. "What other things do they fold?"

"I'll get to that later," he told me darkly, shivering. "Where was I?"

"There he was," I answered, "all fifteen foot of him, standing in the shadows. And then—?"

"A car comes along the street, sudden like!" Bill grabbed my arm.

"Wow!" I jumped. "He's in trouble, right?"

Barmy Bill shook his head. "No way. The car's lights are on full, but that doesn't trouble the thin man. He's not stupid. The car goes by, lighting up the walls with its beam, and where the thin man stood in shadows against the wall of his thin house—"

"Yes?"

"A drainpipe, all black and shiny!"

I sat back. "Pretty smart."

"You better believe they're smart. Then, when it's dark again, out he steps. And *that's* something to see! Those giant strides—but quick, almost a flicker. Blink your eyes and he's moved—and between each movement his legs coming together as he pauses, and nothing to see but a pole. Up to the lamppost he goes, seems almost to melt into it, hides behind it. And *plink*!—out goes the light. After that…in ten minutes he had the whole street black as night in a coalmine. And yours truly lying there in somebody's garden, scared and shivering and dying to throw up."

"And that was it?"

Barmy Bill gulped, tossed back his gin and poured himself another. His eyes were huge now, his skin white where it showed through his whiskers. "God, no—that wasn't it—there was more! See, I figured later that I must have got myself drunk deliberately that time—so's to go up there and spy on 'em. Oh, I know that sounds crazy now, but you know what it's like when you're mindless drunk. Jesus, these days I can't *get* drunk! But these were early days I'm telling you about."

"So what happened next?"

"Next—he's coming back down the street! I can hear him: *click*, pause, *click*, pause...*click,* pause, stilting it along the pavement—and I can see him in my mind's eye, doing his impression of a lamppost with every pause. And suddenly I get this feeling, and I sneak a look round. I mean, the frontage of this garden I'm in is so tiny, and the house behind me is—"

I saw it coming. "Jesus!"

"A thin house," he confirmed it, "right!"

"So now *you* were in trouble."

He shrugged, licked his lips, trembled a little. "I was lucky, I suppose. I squeezed myself into the hedge, lay still as death. And *click*, pause...*click*, pause, getting closer all the time. And then—behind me, for I'd turned my face away—the slow creaking as the door of the thin house swung open! And the second thin person coming out and, I imagine, unfolding him or herself, and the two of 'em standing there for a moment, and me near dead of fright."

"And?"

"*Click-click*, pause; *click-click*, pause; *click-click*—and away they go. God only knows where they went, or what they did, but me?—I gave 'em ten minutes start and then got up, and ran, and stumbled, and forced my rubbery legs to carry me right out of there. And I haven't been back. Why, this is the closest I've been to Barchington since that night, and too close by far!"

I waited for a moment but he seemed done. Finally I nodded. 'Well, that's a good story, Bill, and—"

"I'm not finished!" he snapped. "And it's not just a story..."

"There's more?"

"Evidence," he whispered. "The evidence of your own clever-bugger eyes!"

I waited.

"Go to the window," said Bill, "and peep out through the curtains. Go on, do it."

I did.

"See anything funny?"

I shook my head.

"Blind as a bat!" he snorted. "Look at the street lights—or the absence of lights. I showed you once tonight. They've nicked all the bulbs."

"Kids," I shrugged. "Hooligans. Vandals."

"Huh!" Bill sneered. "Hooligans, here? Unheard of. Vandals? You're joking! What's to vandalize? And when did you last see kids playing in these streets, eh?"

He was right. "But a few missing light bulbs aren't hard evidence," I said.

"All *right*!" he pushed his face close and wrinkled his nose at me. "Hard evidence, then." And he began to tell me the final part of his story...

THREE 3

"Cars!" Barmy Bill snapped, in that abrupt way of his. "They can't bear them. Can't say I blame 'em much, not on that one. I hate the noisy, dirty, clattering things myself. But tell me: have you noticed anything a bit queer—about cars, I mean—in these parts?"

I considered for a moment, replied: "Not a hell of a lot of them."

"Right!" He was pleased. "On the rest of the Hill, nose to tail. Every street overflowing. 'Specially at night when people are in the pubs or watching the telly. But here? Round Barchington and the Larches and a couple of other streets in this neighbourhood? Not a one to be seen!"

"Not true," I said. "There are two cars in this very street right now. Look out the window and you should be able to see them."

"Bollocks!" said Bill.

"Pardon?"

"Bollocks!" he repeated. "Them's not *cars*! Rusting old bangers. Spokewheels and all. Twenty, thirty years they've been trundling about. The thin people are *used* to them. It's the big shiny new ones they don't like. And so, if you park your car up here overnight—trouble!"

"Trouble?" But here I was deliberately playing dumb. Here I knew what he meant well enough. I'd seen it for myself: the occasional shiny car, left overnight, standing there the next morning with its tyres slashed, windows smashed, lamps kicked in.

He could see it in my face. "You know what I mean, all right. Listen, couple of years ago there was a Flash Harry type from the city used to come up here. There was a barmaid he fancied in The Railway—and she was taking all he could give her. Anyway, he was flash, you know? One of the gang lads and a rising star. And a flash car to go with it. Bullet-proof windows, hooded lamps, reinforced panels—the lot. Like a bloody tank, it was. But—" Bill sighed.

"He used to park it up here, right?"

He nodded. "Thing was, you couldn't threaten him, you know what I mean? Some people you can threaten, some you shouldn't threaten, and some you mustn't. He was one you mustn't. Trouble is, so are the thin people."

"So what happened?"

"When they slashed his tyres, he lobbed bricks through their windows. And he had a knowing way with him. He tossed 'em through thin house windows. Then one night he parked down on the corner of Barchington. Next morning—they'd drilled holes right through the plate, all over the car. After that—he didn't come back for a week or so. When he did come back… well, he must've been pretty mad."

"What did he do?"

"Threw something else—something that made a bang! A damn big one! You've seen that thin, derelict shell on the corner of Barchington? Oh, it was him, sure enough, and he got it right, too. A thin house. Anybody in there, they were goners. And *that* did it!"

"They got him?"

"They got his car! He parked up one night, went down to The Railway, when the bar closed took his lady-love back to her place, and in the morning—"

"They'd wrecked it—his car, I mean."

"Wrecked it? Oh, yes, they'd done that. They'd *folded* it!"

"Come again?"

"Folded it!" he snapped. "Their funny science. Eighteen inches each way, it was. A cube of folded metal. No broken glass, no split seams, no splintered plastic. Folded all neat and tidy. An eighteen-inch cube."

"They'd put it through a crusher, surely?" I was incredulous.

"Nope—folded."

"Impossible!"

"Not to them. Their funny science."

"So what did he do about it?"

"Eh? Do? He looked at it, and he thought, 'What if I'd been sitting in the bloody thing?' Do? He did what I would do, what you would do. He went away. We never did see him again."

The half-bottle was empty. We reached for the beers. And after a long pull I said: "You can kip here if you want, on the floor. I'll toss a blanket over you."

"Thanks," said Barmy Bill, "but no thanks. When the beer's gone I'm gone. I wouldn't stay up here to save my soul. Besides, I've a bottle of my own back home."

"Sly old sod!" I said.

"Daft young bugger!" he answered without malice. And twenty minutes later I let him out. Then I crossed to the windows and looked out at him, at the street all silver in moonlight.

He stood at the gate (where it should be) swaying a bit and waving up at me, saying his thanks and farewell. Then he started off down the street.

It was quiet out there, motionless. One of those nights when even the trees don't move. Everything frozen, despite the fact that it wasn't nearly cold. I watched Barmy Bill out of sight, craning my neck to see him go, and—

Across the road, three lampposts—where there should only be two! The one on the left was OK, and the one to the far right. But the one in the middle? I had never seen that one before. I blinked bleary eyes, gasped, blinked again. Only *two* lampposts!

Stinking drunk—drunk as a skunk—utterly boggled!

I laughed as I tottered from the window, switched off the light, staggered into my bedroom. The barmy old bastard had really had me going. I'd really started to believe. And now the booze was making me see double—or something. Well, just as long as it was lampposts and not pink elephants! Or thin people! And I went to bed laughing.

...But I wasn't laughing the next morning.

Not after they found him, old Barmy Bill of Barrows Hill. Not after they called on me to identify him.

"Their funny science," he'd called it. The way they folded things. And Jesus, they'd folded him, too! Right down into an eighteen-inch cube. Ribs and bones and skin and muscles—the lot. Nothing broken, you understand, just folded. No blood or guts or anything nasty—nastier by far *because* there was nothing.

And they'd dumped him in a garbage-skip at the end of the street. The couple of local youths who found him weren't even sure what they'd found, until they spotted his face on one side of the cube. But I won't go into that...

WELL, I MOVED out of there just as soon as I could—do you blame me?—since when I've done a lot of thinking about it. Fact is, I haven't thought of much else.

And I suppose old Bill was right. At least I hope so. Things he'd told me earlier, when I was only half listening. About them being the last of their sort, and Barrows Hill being the place they've chosen to sort of fade away in, like a thin person's 'elephant's graveyard,' you know?

Anyway, there are no thin people here, and no thin houses. Vandals aplenty, and so many cars you can't count, but nothing out of the ordinary.

Lampposts, yes, and posts to hold up the telephone wires, of course. Lots of them. But they don't bother me anymore.

See, I know *exactly* how many lampposts there are. And I know exactly *where* they are, every last one of them. And God help the man who ever plants a new one without telling me first!

Stilts
Stilts

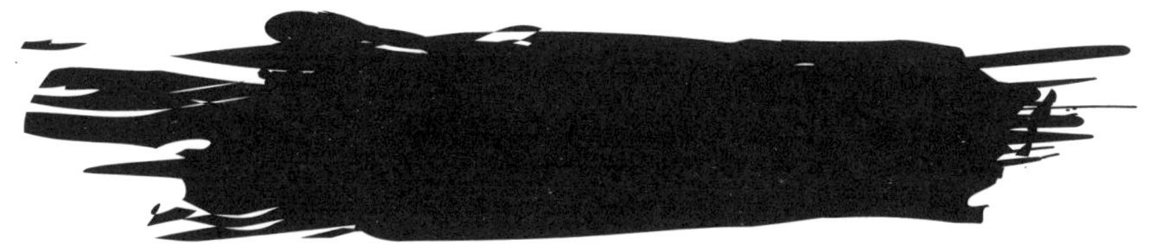

EAR DIARY—

Yes, it's me again…I bet you thought I'd died, right? But no, I just went away for a while; or rather I got away. It was a bad case of GAFIA: Getting Away From It All. Mainly from London, from Barrows Hill and the Thin People.

I thought I had forgotten about the Thin People; I *tried* to forget about them, putting them down to my temporary addiction, my "penchant" for alcohol. Incidentally, that was why I started corresponding with you, Diary…I thought, maybe if I told it all to you, maybe if I described how well I was getting on, how I was winning over my, er, "urge"—in fact my compulsion—to imbibe almost every-damn-thing from beer to mouthwash to ciggy-lighter fuel, that would be much better than bearing my booze-sodden soul to some tooth-tapping trick-cyclist, some shrunken shrink, some fingernail-munching counsellor, some pallid pack of lying Alcoholics Anonymous groupies, and like that.

In fact—on looking back—it was just such cynicism that kept me from these barely possible remedies; that and the fact that I considered myself "strong," hated to admit my addiction to anyone other than myself…and to you, of course.

And the thing is I honestly can't remember whether or not I was in trouble with my drinking *before* Barrows Hill and the Thin People, or if it came on later. If it was before, then I might be able to say that everything that happened was simply an attack of the dreaded dt's; might even dismiss the episode entirely. But on the other hand I can't seem to recall a previous problem. Or maybe that's just how it catches up with you, by stealth. But if it was *after* Barrows Hill—

—Well, that's what worries me.

Okay, Diary, I accept that I was a drinker—in fact some kind of drinking fool—but not until after she'd dumped me.

She, yes…

A little less than three and a half years ago, Diary, you were made up of page after page about her. Until she left and I ripped them out, burned them to ashes, and buried the ashes in the old lady's garden downstairs, like some kind of grave. And if I hadn't got out of Barrows Hill…well, who knows? Maybe I'd still be grieving and putting down flowers on that grave even now. But I did get out, because of the Thin People. And because of what happened to Barmy Bill.

The Thin People, who came out of their thin houses at night to do their thing—"tea-leafing," thieving, as old Barmy Bill of

Barrows Hill, the old codger who told me about them, called it. And where's Barmy Bill now, eh? Either he had the weirdest, most inexplicable and horrible accident of all time—to end up square like that, an eighteen inch cube with his flattened face on one side—or the Thin People did it to him after he talked to me. And at the time, I wasn't willing to take the chance.

Accident? I didn't think so. Thin People? Well, the trouble is I *thought* I'd seen one of them...maybe. So they were either real or it was a bad case of the dt's. Whichever, it had scared me enough I packed my bags (plastic bags, that is) and portable typewriter, and got out.

And as for Lois or Lori or Lorraine (shit, I can't even be sure of her name now) I've done almost as good a job of forgetting her as I *thought* I had done of forgetting the Thin People. So may your poor buried ashes rest in peace, Diary.

But as for the Thin People—

—I hate to admit this, but there have been reminders...

Diaries go year by year, usually. And so do you, Diary. Or you should but you're three years out of date, just a notebook now. Still, what the hell, I can talk to you because you're not a shrink and you can't talk back. Or maybe you can.

Let's turn one or two of your pages back to find that time I took a holiday in Cyprus. The sun, the sea, and the sand. And no booze. I was over it. I had a good job up in the north-east, Newcastle, and I was in control. All those bars, those alfresco tavernas—all that cheap Keo beer in big brown bottles—that Metaxa, clear Ouzo, dusty *resinata*? Hell, no! No way! Make mine a diet Coke. Water, even. How clean can you get?

And I would look at the holidaymakers in the Cypriot night—all tipsy, some stoned, others flat out—and think, "God, what clowns we make of ourselves!" But now, when I think about clowns, I think of something else.

Clowns: they used to scare me as a kid and still do, even more now. But I'll get to that.

Out there in Cyprus, however, well it was a great holiday. Only one thing spoiled it; one little nothing kind of thing, a dream I had that turned into something else. And here it is as I wrote it down in your pages, Diary:

…I think I was dreaming about those Thin People that Barmy Bill told me about—I think I probably dream of them quite frequently, but can't remember too much about it when I'm awake. Just as well, I suppose. Old Bill told me they looked a lot like men in the daylight—not that they were out very much in the daylight—but that at night they were more themselves. At night they unfolded *themselves, like a joiner's wooden ruler but fifteen feet long and incredibly thin. He said it was their science, totally different from ours, which let them manipulate matter differently. That was how they could do things with their bodies; even with… well,* other *bodies. Bill said their joints must be similar to the joints of certain insects…*

So that's what I was thinking, or dreaming, as I came awake in my hammock under the grapevines, in the garden of the hotel where I was staying, near the British military base in Dhekelia. Or was it?

Perhaps what I saw as I slowly woke up reminded me of that time in Barrows Hill. So that I wasn't so much dreaming as reflecting—constructing or maybe reconstructing one event from the other—until both events merged, flowing into each other in the surreal interval between true dreaming and full consciousness.

But as for what I actually saw *as I awakened…well, that was more dreamlike than a dream! In fact, and if I didn't know it now to be a natural phenomenon, I would have to say it was nightmarish.*

Who am I kidding, it was *nightmarish!*

Close by. In the cropped grass, I noticed that a small area of the ground was moving…

Now consider: the place where I was staying was rather rare on a Mediterranean island, insofar as the garden had real grass. And the owner was very proud of it. He watered it daily and cut it twice a week—despite that it didn't need it. I saw him watering and cutting away at it that morning. Maybe that's what caused it, made the earth damp and brought about a disturbance.

Anyway, a small patch of ground nearby was moving. And lying there on my side in the netting—surfacing from what was probably a deep sleep—I saw a run of cropped grass blades parting as the soil beneath them bulged upward, forming a hummock three or four inches long and two across.

Then the earth broke open, and this thing nosed its way out. Emerging slowly at first—shaking the soil off its furry little body—it came out, and I knew at once what it was. It was a mole! Or at least the first part of it was, the first couple of inches.

But a mole with antennae?

And I think I can be forgiven for believing that I was still asleep and dreaming…because then the rest of it pushed its way out.

Okay, those first couple of inches: I saw these legs—mole legs, covered with bristling fur—then the dark hairy snout, and a furry mole body. So far so good. But not really. Because sticking out from the snout were these antennae, and halfway down the mole body was an oddly jointed pair of insect *legs! And if I hadn't been awake before, well I certainly was by then.*

The rest of the body emerged—the thorax, as I now know it to have been. No fur, just three inches of unpleasantness, of long, folded-back spiky-tipped wings, and another pair of those thorny insect legs. Until finally it was out in the open.

I looked at it wide-eyed, and this thing looked back at me, through eyes like tiny red faceted beads. Then it shook itself one last time, opened its wings and flew. I heard the whirring—ducked as it seemed to come right at me—almost fell out of my hammock as it buzzed close overhead…

Later I spoke to Costas, the owner of the hotel. He laughed when I told him how I'd nearly fallen…and he told me what I'd seen: a mole cricket. There weren't too many of them, but neither were they very rare. My opinion: those nightmarish little bastards should *be rare! And extinct would be even better…!*

…Back home, I checked it out in a book at the library. A mole cricket, sure enough—genus Gryllotalpa*—an "injurious insect." Well, the damn thing very nearly injured me, for sure!*

So THERE YOU go, Diary: a flash-back of sorts, reminding me of those Thin People in Barrows Hill who might or might not have been a result of my drinking. Except now I'm pretty sure they weren't. I mean, there are so many things in the earth—and on this Earth—that we don't know about. Okay, so people know about mole crickets. *Some* people do, even if I didn't. But what if there are other things, species that are unknown, that no one has ever seen? Or if they have seen them, did they know what they were seeing? And I'm not just talking about the Thin People…

So what am I talking about, eh, Diary? Well, it's this new thing. Except (God help me) I'd been drinking again, and can't really be sure. But I'm pretty sure…

A FAIR WAS in town. Now usually, these days, a fair is no big deal. In England they've sort of dried up, lost a lot of their appeal; not to kids—no, of course not—but among parents. I mean, who can afford them any more? The rides and sideshows are too expensive, and you need a cast-iron stomach to handle the greasy rubbish they sell from the fast-food stalls. What's more, it's a very rare fair that doesn't attract rain. It can be bright and summery in the morning—"autumnal" in the case in question—but from the moment those big artics and painted wagons start rolling in, look out! Here come the thunderheads.

This fair, however, was unusual. It came annually, in late August or early September, and was as big as any three standard fairs rolled up in one…because it *was* three fairs joined up and working as one, creating what the proprietors knew would be a big local attraction on one of their last gigs of the season. Big, garish and very noisy, yes. Flashing lights, tubular neons and coloured balloons; the rumble of generators versus a calliope; the smell of grease, friction, sawdust; the hoarse-voiced Loreleis at hoopla stalls and coconut-shies, all of them vying with each other to lure you to financial doom; the penny slots, Ghost Train, Freak House, Hall of Mirrors—the whole bit.

I say the fair was "in town" but in fact it was in a field on the outskirts, the same field every year. For several weeks I'd been noticing (barely) the big bright posters. They hadn't made much of an impact; wrapped up in my work, everything else was peripheral. But last Friday morning on my way into town on the bus, as I passed the field in question, I saw the first of the artics starting to arrive. Down the road there was a long string of them. And not a cloud in sight. It made a change.

Saturday morning, a friend of mine called me. Just out of bed, I answered the phone. "It's George," he told me. "Haven't seen you in a month of Sundays! Watcha doing these days? Still tied up with your big-deal, high-pressure job? Still doing the cub reporter bit—that 'Superman's pal, Jimmy Olson' sort of thing?"

"If you mean am I still a journalist? Yes. No big deal; I just like to write, that's all."

George was an interior decorator…that's what he called himself, but all he did really was patch over cracked ceilings with wavy-patterned, quick-drying cement stuff, and then paint it to make it look good.

"Me?" George answered. "I'm free this weekend, and I wondered if you were, too."

As it happened, I was. "So what do you have in mind?"

"There's this girl I'm seeing," he said. "She's really sort of nice. Has a nice friend, too. So what do you say to a double date? The big fair's in town, out my way, and I was thinking we could get together with the girls. Maybe have a few drinks, buy them some candy floss, win 'em a fluffy toy on the rifle range, maybe take 'em for a ride, and then—who knows? Take 'em for another ride? Know what I mean, nudge, nudge?"

I knew George and his girls of old. "You want to fix me up with a girl? Does she wear a collar? Is her bark worse than her bite? Has she won a prize at Crufts? Know what I mean—nudge, nudge?"

"Hey!" He tried to sound hurt. "That's not nice. Gloria's a really sweet girl. Also, a little bird told me she does a terrific horizontal snake dance."

"What little bird?"

"My little bird, Gladys."

I had seen George's Gladys, and she really was quite a good looking girl. "So how does this Gloria compare—with Gladys, I mean?"

"They could be sisters." (The liar!) "So, what do you say?"

"As to the girls: why not? As to the drinking: you know I'm off it."

"So drink something non-toxic! I mean, it's not like you're a genuine, died-in-the-wool alcoholic, now is it?"

I still liked to pretend I wasn't, or hadn't been, and so I said okay.

We all make mistakes, Diary. And you know me. I make really big ones…

SUNDAY THE FAIRGROUND was all set up, ready to roll that night. I met George and the girls at eight o'clock at a little pub not a quarter mile from the fair. Pausing on the street just before I entered the place, I could hear a low near-distant rumble and the shrill squeals of people on the rides. The fair's rotating, zigzagging, strobing lights were plainly visible in the gathering dusk.

Apart from George and the girls the pub was almost empty. I joined them in a small booth at a grubby table where a pint was sitting waiting for me, the froth still fresh and deep. No good to reproach George; after all, I was the one who had told him I could take it or leave it, that I was only a social drinker. In fact it was something of a relief to take that first sip and to lick the foam off my upper lip. And despite that they knew they shouldn't, my spirits were lifting even as I sighed a paradoxically reticent yet appreciative oh-what-the-hell sort of sigh. What was it Barmy Bill had called me that weird night in Barrows Hill? A "daft young sod?" He wasn't so Barmy, poor Bill…

After that…well, things just got sillier by the minute. I don't know why I let it happen; maybe I believed in that old saw about girls getting more desirable the more drunk you get; which where this Gloria was concerned was going to take a whole lot of booze, believe me! But before I knew it, it was my round, then George's, then mine again, and so on. Stupid, really. And Gloria didn't get any prettier.

Diary, I'm not going to describe George, Gladys, or Gloria, (let's just call them the Three "G"s) because that's not what I want to write about—they were simply the reason why I visited the fairground that night—so excuse me if they get left in a remote part of what has since become my rather blurry memories, and instead of trying to fill in all the blanks I'll simply cut to the chase, okay?

The fairground:

Now this year it was really big, and probably bigger in my slightly altered perceptions. Only slightly altered, yes. See, Diary, when I've got drink in me I don't start raving—I just don't think very well, that's all. I can still walk a straight line… approximately. And I can still speak properly…well, more or less; so that folks who don't know me too well probably wouldn't know the difference. But *I* know it: that dull-numb-stupid feeling inside my head, that sure knowledge that I'm no longer in control, and that I don't care. And I also know that if I go on not caring, then sooner or later I'll do something, or something will be done to me, that will land me in a whole lot of trouble. It's the reason I don't drive a car. Though I intend to, one day, when I'm sure…

And then there's the other side of it: the fact that once you've fallen off the wagon, it's no easy job to climb back on again. Which in me leads to anger, because I like to think I'm stronger than that. And I am, *I bloody well am*! It's just that everything seems to go wrong, seems to work against you, until you've put it all back to rights again.

So that, too: I was angry. Not so much with the Three "G"s as with myself. And there I was "suddenly" in this fairground, my head spinning just a little—and pissed with myself, with that weak area in my psyche which had failed to stop me at the first pungent whiff of a good brew—and the whirling lights, hurtling machines, clinking slots and jostling crowd not doing me a hell of a lot of good either. I think I remember thinking to myself, "Thank God it isn't raining!"

The Three "G"s tried to lure me onto a gut-wrenching, whirling dervish of a ride. I knew that I'd throw up, and then that I'd feel wretched; so when they went aboard I made off, breathing as deeply as I could of the smoky, trembling air.

I remember burning my mouth and fingers on a plastic cup of coffee at a hot dog stand. And shortly after that—

—There it was in front of me: the Freak Show tent.

The freaks (they weren't freaks really, just poor misshapen or peculiarly strange and ugly people—which on afterthought pretty much qualifies them as freaks, right? Oh, well!) weren't drawing very much of an audience, so a handful of them had come out to parade in the night air and chat up the crowd. There was a Fat Lady who truly deserved the title; she was several inches wider than she was tall, which was around four feet six. Swaddled in diapers that were once tablecloths, under a frilly tutu of a dress, the wobbling slabs of flesh that depended from her thighs and buttocks hung almost to the ground. I could see she was feeling peckish, because her shining, vastly pouting Cupid lips were sucking on a whole stick of butter dipped in sugar.

There was no Thin Man—I was glad to note—but there was a Strong Man. His arms bulged massively on a frame reminiscent of a Challenger tank. But on the other hand his rather suspect legs were hidden in floppy track-suit pants. (No weight-lifter this one, I thought, not with his sparrow legs…but I certainly wouldn't want to take him on at arm-wrestling.)

And then there was a girl contortionist in black and silver tights, walking on her hands with her feet behind her neck. She would "walk" a few paces in this mode, then pause and swing her body to and fro like one of those rocking plastic birds pecking at water. She worked this up to such a pitch that I thought her face would surely smack into the earth with the next swing; but after she got down close enough to snatch up a dandelion flower between her teeth, then she was done. And uncoiling herself, she proceeded to hop around on one foot while hugging the other leg vertically in front of her, its knee up under her chin and the toes on its foot pointing at the sky.

And finally there was the Tattooed Man, who also played the part of team barker. Now, I had seen his sort before, but never one with as many tattoos as this. On a spare, loose-limbed body not a single inch of space was wasted; he looked like the Illustrated Man from that story by Ray Bradbury. I was fascinated by the animals, the faces, the designs, the mazes, the colours. He was young; he'd spent half his life under the needle; he was *in himself* an art form and a graffiti gallery combined!

These weird people…just looking at them…it was all so strange, so startling, so dizzying, that in combination with the beer it set my head to spinning again, though at the time I had thought the fumes were beginning to clear.

The time…? How long had I been at the fair, anyway?

In the dazed, uncomprehending fashion of a man who has had too much to drink, I studied my watch: a little after ten twenty. Me and the Three "G"s had left the pub, oh, around nine, so I had been here for something over an hour. No sign of my erstwhile companions. But then again, who needed them? And that was definitely the booze speaking. I'm not normally that dismissive of my friends.

And the tattooed barker was up on a box shouting, "…cheap at half the price! So come on in, sir, madame, lads and lasses, and see us do our stuff. See the Monkey Lady, Jimmy the Legless Boy, Freddy the Fly, and Bela the Human Pincushion. Plus me and the gang here, all with new things to show you. As for myself—why, I could show you tattoos that even my wife hasn't seen! So roll up, roll up! It's cheap at half the price! Your money back if you aren't completely astonished! Come on and take a chance, and be amazed when you visit the weirdest show on Earth!"

The Freak Show tent was on the outer rim of the fair, which was probably why it wasn't attracting too much attention. There was something of a small crowd, but its people had only come on the scene to see what all the shouting was about. The center of the fair blazed with light and activity, like the hub of a miniature star-cluster. Here on the outer rim, however, where there was more space between the wagons, tents, and kiddy rides, this was more like the galaxy's spiral arm: the light was dimmer and the shadows longer. And beyond this outer circle—there where the field reached out toward open country—that was like deep space, as dark as the hour.

Looking up, the stars above the center were faint, made dim by light pollution; here on the rim there was something more of a sparkle to them; outside the fair's perimeter, they were like jewels strewn on black velvet. There was nothing to distinguish the sky from the earth…the night was a sea of darkness, or a wall of fine black mesh that rose on high, sprinkled with stars in its upper regions.

As I stared at one small cluster of stars, they momentarily vanished—just the slightest blink of an eye—and as quickly reappeared. I supposed that a cloud, or perhaps a waft of fairground exhaust, had passed between. But then there was movement out there, too, in the smoky velvet darkness between the tents.

The barker was still shouting the wares of the Freak House; his "gang" were doing their strange things; a girl with a small yappy dog was dodging in and out and around the legs of parties come to observe, trying to find a better viewpoint. And without warning, suddenly the clown was there…but he was surely the crowned King of Clowns!

I don't know where he came from…he could only have come from outside—probably from the night-side of the tent, where some other member of the Freaks had helped him up onto his gear—but the way he appeared was like magic.

Which was only right; for fairgrounds and Freak Shows and such, well they're supposed to be magic, aren't they? But whether or no, there he was, this clown on stilts, as colourful as the circus he belonged in, his head as high as the tent's ridge-pole.

The crowd *oohed*! and *aahed*! as he stilted carefully between groups. And a curious thing: the other performers—all four of them—they seemed equally taken aback by his presence.

"Wow!" I said, moving close to the Strong Man. "Surely he's too tall for the tent?"

"Eh?" The huge fellow cast me a frowning glance. "What, our tent? Oh, no, he's not one of ours. In fact I didn't know there were more of our kind here." He nodded his great, bearded head. "He's from one of the other fairs, for sure. But hey! He's welcome if he helps draw in the crowd! Absolutely!"

And as the Strong Man moved off, I stood there admiring the clown on stilts; stood there swaying just a little, still dizzy with drink and fairground motion, as the people seemed to swirl around me, occasionally jostling me aside.

Apart from his great long stilts the clown was more or less typical of his breed…more or less. He effected a great red beak rather than one of those squashy noses; his tall, pork-pie hat sprouted green feathers; he wore a shiny black swallow-tail coat, its ridiculously long, stiff, curved tails hanging almost to where his feet must be situated inside narrow, horizontally-striped, green and grey pipe-stem trousers. The trousers seemed gathered at the "ankle" of the stilts, whose "feet" were three-clawed triangles of black plastic or painted wood…whichever, they were as shiny as patent leather shoes. And large? It could only be that these size fifteen pontoons helped him to balance.

The clown was blackfaced, hugely white-lipped under the beak, and wore red goggle-eyes that reflected the rotating, near-distant lights of the rides. His thin neck was enclosed in a green collar of some furry material, and he wore green gloves on slim, long-fingered hands. At his hips his trousers bulged awkwardly, "clownishly," of course, and I assumed that these bulges hid or disguised the upper extremes of his stilts and whatever mechanism allowed him to bend his legs where his feet (now his clown knees) would be. Without doubt his was a clever get-up, despite that his jerking movements must be hellishly difficult to orchestrate.

The young girl with the yappy dog was one of the main jostlers. "I can't see, I can't see!" she was muttering, tugging at my elbow. "Mister, can I get in front?" But as I let her get by me she dropped the dog's lead. And off he went, straight as the proverbial arrow to his target: the Freaks where they clustered around the new kid on the block.

"Woofy, come *back* here!" the girl, maybe nine or ten years old (God only knows what she was doing out on her own—or with the dog—so late at night!) cried after him. But Woofy wasn't listening. Excited, and like myself fascinated, he was going to get as close as doggily possible to these peculiar people.

I detected an odour. But…there are smells and there are smells. And sometimes they'll bring back memories of events you thought were long forgotten. Like that time when I was a little kid and my lips were chapped. A girl I fancied at school loaned me this clear lip-salve in a propelling lipstick-like tube; its smell was not quite peppermint, and I've never come across that smell again. But the moment I think of that little girl, everything comes back to me as clear as yesterday—especially that smell.

That was a nice thing; other things aren't. For example:

I remember another time from my childhood, and in fact from another fairground, but this one in the spring when I was maybe as young as the girl with the dog. It was the year of the cockchafer, the May bug. At least I think that's what they were. Me and my lot, the kids I knocked about with, had our own name for them: we called them shit-beetles, because of the stench if you crushed one. And they were big, nasty, *flying* shit-beetles.

I had this friend, Stanley. Even as a child and long before pubescence he was plagued with acne, pimples, boils, whelkiness in general. And Stanley had some money! We penniless kids could only look on in envy while Stanley whirled on high, flung round and round in his Flying Chair. But as the ride began to slow he was crying; and as the centrifugal force lessened and his chair fell from the near-horizontal to the vertical, where Stanley's feet touched down on the ride's boards, he was disgusting!

He must have flown through a cloud of the things—because he had shit-beetles splattered all over him. And Stanley stank! I remember someone remarking, "Hey, don't worry about it, Stan. Let's face it, you don't look any worse than before!" You know, kids can be cruel like that.

But there you go: I only have to recall that fairground, on that day, and poor Stanley, and I remember the smell, the shit-beetle smell. In fact *this* smell, or one very much like it. Too much like it.

I looked around. Close by, the pink face of a child-in-arms was half lost in a huge ball of sticky candy floss. And another was licking a toffee-apple that was about to fall off its stick. So was that it? A combination of stinks? And the kid in diapers—the one with the toffee-apple—had he or she just shat? God, I felt ill!

The smell went away, drifted in another direction, and once again I focused on the clown on stilts. The Tattooed Man, still on his box, was looking up at him, talking to him. "What's your outfit, my friend? I mean, I hate to poach, but we could definitely do with someone like you!" But then he frowned and curled his lip. "Or maybe you're here for another reason—not to lend a hand but to lure the crowd away! Well, what do you say?"

The clown looked down, shrugged, and shook his head. He was either dumb—or playing dumb, like other clowns I've seen—or he simply didn't understand. What, a foreign clown?

And waddling closer, the Fat Lady piped up, "Hey, give the man a break! Maybe he's in that Russian circus. They're playing in Sunderland. It's odds-on he's come to catch our act, see how we perform." She held up a pudgy hand. "How're you doing, pal?"

The clown on stilts cocked his head on one side, gazed down at her upturned face, bent over and sniffed at her. It was part of his act, obviously. First he played dumb, and then he played daft. The Fat Lady laughed and said, "I smell good, right?" And she held up her hand higher yet. He took it, she shook it, they slowly let go; and looking oddly puzzled—jerking his head in an almost robotic fashion—the clown straightened up again.

But that amazing bending action! How in hell had he managed that? His stilts must be the most marvelous contraptions, that he could bend as low as that without toppling over. And if this fellow was typical of his comrades, well that Russian circus in Sunderland must be one very class act!

Meanwhile, Woofy was having the time of his doggy life. In and out like a mad thing; up on his hind legs one minute, down on all fours the next; his front legs stiff and jerking in time with his barking, and his hind-quarters stuck up in the air. It was all in fun, though, for his tail was wagging fit to tip him over. Then, a mistake. Someone trod on his paw and Woofy, overexcited, snapped much too close to an ankle.

A cry of outrage, followed immediately by a swift kick that grazed Woofy's rump, causing him to yelp. In a flash his little mistress was there to snatch him up out of harm's way.

Someone yelled, "Get that bloody dog out of here!" And flying to the back of the crowd, the young girl (who for the first time I saw to be a scruffy, raggedy child with a stubborn, pouting mouth) turned with Woofy in her arms and shouted, "Fuck you, shit-face!" Ah, childhood! Ah, innocence! Ah, bollocks!

Someone cried, "Smile, please!" And a flashbulb went off in a brief, brilliant starburst. I blinked in sympathy; and on his stilts, waving his arms before his face, the clown backed off a pace. He'd had his picture taken, but *my* after-image was one of the Fat Lady looking distinctly nauseous, pulling a face as she wiped her hand on her taffeta tutu.

My vision cleared. The crowd had thickened. A man was holding his obese child—the one with the toffee-apple—up to the clown on stilts. The child was giggling, kicking, and trying to lick all at the same time. The apple fell off its stick and the child quickly sobered. Deprived, its expression changed, became anxious; its mouth trembled, puckered up, shaped a grating wail of distress that rapidly built to a shriek.

Oh no, no, no! Tut-tut-tut! The clown took the child in two hands, bounced it in mid-air, a gentle vertical shaking motion, almost as if he were weighing that small, fat, crappy bundle on a pair of sprung scales. Then, cocking his head at that curious angle again, he leaned forward and returned the screaming child to its father; while a woman—the mother, maybe?—scrambled to grab up the now filthy apple and ram it back on its stick.

The smell—*that* smell—hit me again, stronger this time, and suddenly, out of nowhere, a whole string of pictures, vivid as life, went flashing across my mind:

Ploukie Stanley, head down and sobbing into his pullover as his Flying Chair slowed to a halt; the mole cricket's squirming as it emerged from its burrow; Barmy Bill's flattened face on a perfectly compacted eighteen-inch cube of flesh.

And again I felt sick as a dog, a volcanic surge of liquids rising in my gut, threatening to erupt. Out of the now thinning crowd I stumbled—out between a pair of wagons vibrating with the rumble and roar of their generators—out into the darkness and the night and the open field.

I lurched against a fence; the top bar was hanging loose; I sat on the center bar and leaned forward, knowing from my heaving guts exactly what was going to happen—and exactly *why* it would happen. It was my pills, of course! It wasn't just that I *shouldn't* drink, but that I *couldn't* drink! For eighteen months now I had been taking this medication, just one pill each morning, to prohibit my drinking. There are no side effects, unless you drink. If you drink you throw up, horribly! But in eighteen months it had become a habit in itself—and I'd forgotten all about it. This morning, as usual, I had taken a pill, and right now I was about to pay for my forgetfulness, for having drunk a forbidden drink. What, just one little drink? Hell no, at least four pints of beer! On top of the pill and the day's meals…and everything burning like acid, searing my insides as it came surging for the surface. Oh, joy!

Diary, I'm not going to describe the next fifteen minutes. It was probably no more than that, but it felt like an hour and a half. And the fairground throbbing away to match my throbbing head; and halfway through, something at my feet that wagged its stumpy tail and sniffed tentatively at the mess that lay steaming on the grass down there.

And I thought, *God, don't eat that, little fellow*!

Time passed unnoticed…

And while I sat there on the broken fence—propped against a post with my head down, shoulders slumped, and hands dangling—wishing I was dead, I sensed him there.

The tall fellow. The clown on stilts. I tried to look up, but my vision was blurred, made misty by reason of my watering eyes. In the near-distance the fairground was like some foggy Xanadu, like a luminous pavilion floating on a black velvet sea. And silhouetted darkly against its soft glow, this tall, tall figure, as motionless as some freakish scarecrow in the night.

I saw him there, however dimly, but even without seeing him I would have sensed him, would have known his smell. And my pal Woofy knew it, too. Off he went, zigzagging and yapping, stiff-legged and bouncing, making more noise than you'd believe possible from such a small creature, into the darkness. And as for me: I threw up again…

Something brought me out of it. I don't know what it was; a sound, perhaps? A cry, a yelp, a brittle snapping, the sound of crunching bones? I can't say, but something.

I still couldn't stand, and so clung to my post. And there in the night I saw a strange thing. No, let me try that again—I *thought* I saw, and heard, a strange thing: a shadow, flitting on high, whirring as it passed overhead. A winged shape, like a great dragonfly, clutching a small still bundle in its weirdly-jointed appendages. Then a sudden, sharp swerve—the plangent sound of plucked telephone wires where they were strung between tall poles—and silence. But not for long.

"Woofy! Woofy! Where *are* you, Woofy?" The rude, ragged girl-child, running under the stars, sobbing, searching in some kind of frenzied desperation. She raced across the field, her shrill voice gradually fading into the distance, until I was left with my thoughts where I sat shivering, but no longer from sickness, and certainly not from any physical chill. And the thought uppermost in my mind, which even then I couldn't or didn't want to pursue or explore or explain, was this:

You're not going to find Woofy, you snotty little girl. No, I don't think you're ever going to find Woofy...

AND DIARY, THAT'S just about it. We're almost done.

Eventually I was able to stand up again, by which time the fairground's lights were going out, its main generators silent. Then, remembering—things—I looked across the field. Darkness, nothing, now. But in my mind's eye pictures were forming, and they were such that I knew I'd never rid my memory of them:

The stilt-clown's too long tail-coat, with its stiff, shiny-black swallow-tails. The way he had handled his stilts, *if* they were stilts. And the way he'd smelled...for surely the stench had been his? Worse still, the picture in my mind of him weighing that overfed, shrieking infant...which he might well have considered too heavy for his fell purpose. For even poor little Woofy had proved to be a problem, *weighing him down and causing him to run afoul of the telephone cables*!

Those last two were the thoughts that did it: chilled me to the bone and sent me running, stumbling to the roadside where I flagged down a taxi to carry me home. But I couldn't sleep. And yet—just like that earlier episode in Barrows Hill—

neither could I be sure, not even then, not one hundred per cent *sure*, that it wasn't the drink or my warped imagination or…or…or I didn't know what else!

Which is why, Diary, I called in Monday morning to tell my boss I was ill but I'd be in a.s.a.p., then went out and caught a bus back to the fairground. And wouldn't you know it? It was raining, and the place was as drab and unwelcoming as any fairground in the rain. But far more so to me. Frighteningly so, to me.

Hands in pockets, I wandered among the rides and stalls and wagons, just me and a bunch of urchins who must have been playing truant from the local schools. The only thing that was open was a slots arcade, where two tiny old ladies were arguing over whose go it was on one of those claw machines, though what they would do with one of the hideous fluffy toy prizes—if or when they won one—was anybody's guess.

Eventually I made my way to the Freak Show tent, closed for the day, whose sodden eaves dripped rain on the flattened grass and whose gangway floorboards oozed mud. I looked through a gap in the tarpaulin door but there was no sign of the Freaks themselves.

And finally I did what I had to do—what I'd come here to do—and walked out between the perimeter wagons into the empty field. Over there, the fence with the broken rail; and there on the grass, a slimy looking solidified soup which I no more than glanced at because that might set me off again.

And nearby, there on the ground under the looping telephone cables, something limp and wet and furry. At first

I thought it might be Woofy, but it wasn't. Six or seven inches long by four wide, it had fur or hair of a sort, yes—but nothing that ever came from a dog.

For the fur, set on a backing of thin chitin or pearly grey overlapping scales, was striped grey and green...horizontally, I believe. And it stank like poor Stanley when he came down off those Flying Chairs.

DIARY, I MAKE no claim to understand any of this. No claim whatsoever...That's probably because I'm drinking again and can't seem to think straight...Or maybe I'm just too sensitive, too easily disturbed.

I mean, I really don't *want* to understand it, you know?

I don't want to, but I think I do...

The Nonesuch

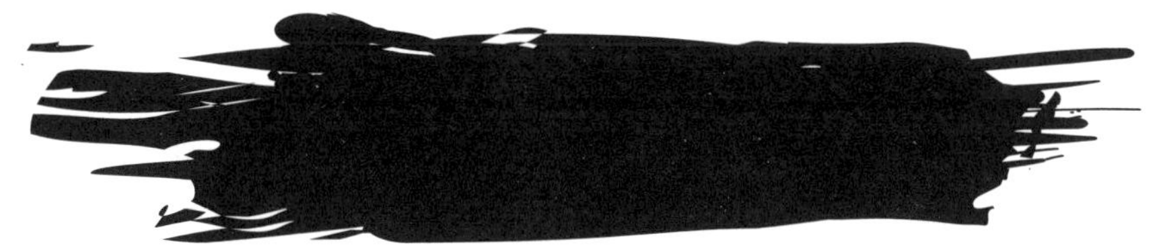

I've often heard it said that lightning never strikes twice. Oh really? Then how about three times? Or perhaps, in some unknown fashion, I'm some kind of unusually prominent lightning conductor whose prime function is to absorb something of the physical and psychological shocks of these *by no means rare* events, thus shielding the rest of humanity and keeping them out of the line of fire. Something like that, anyway.

Or there again perhaps not. My being there didn't much help Barmy Bill of Barrows Hill that time in old London Town. It was more like I was an observer…except even now I can't be sure of what I saw, what really happened. Perhaps I was drinking too much, in which case it could have been a very bad attack of the dreaded delirium tremens. That's what I tell myself anyway, because it's a whole lot easier than recalling to mind the actual details of that morning when the police required me to identify Barmy Bill's dramatically—in fact his radically, *hideously*—altered body where it had been dumped in that skip on Barchington, just off The Larches…

Anyway, let's stop there, because that's another story and somewhere I really don't want to go, not in any detail. But if we're still talking lightning strikes, then Barmy Bill and the Thin People would be numero uno's Numero Uno: my personal Number One, my first but by no means my last.

Or maybe we should be talking something else. There's this dictionary definition that comes to mind: "nonesuch: a *unique*, unparalleled or extraordinary thing." And if we break that down into its component parts:

"Unique." But doesn't that describe a one-off? So how many nonesuches are there supposed to be? I mean is a nonesuch, like a lightning strike, only supposed to occur once? Well not in my case, brother! No, not at all in my case. But as for "unparalleled" and "extraordinary thing(s)": those at least are parts of the definition that I can go along with. But definitely.

Putting it simply, there are some weird things in this old world, and then there are some *really* weird things—nonesuches of a different colour, as it were—and it seems to me that indeed I am destined to attract or collide with them. Not so much a lightning conductor as a magnet, maybe? Or perhaps the weirdness itself is the magnet and I'm simply an iron filing, unable to escape its attraction.

High-flown, fanciful analogies? Well, perhaps…

Anyway and whichever, the nightmarish fate of Barmy Bill of Barrows Hill at the hands of the Thin People was one such occurrence—my first collision with a nonesuch or nonesuches, so to speak—which seems almost to have been instrumental in jarring the rest of these things into monstrous motion...

I USED TO keep a diary, but no longer...because it's not easy to forget things once you write them down. And there are things I would much prefer to forget.

So why am I writing this? Well, maybe I'm hoping it will be cathartic, that I'll purge myself of some of the after-effects, the lingering emotional baggage and psychoses—especially the nightmares and constant panic attacks—the fear, even in broad daylight, that something terrifying knows who I am, and where I live, and might be waiting for me just around the next corner.

You see, no sooner had I got—or thought I had got—Barmy Bill's weird fate out of my mind, my system, than up popped the next nonesuch: the Clown on Stilts. I had been drinking again—"under the influence of my peers," as we frequently tend to excuse ourselves—and so, once again, I can't be one hundred per cent sure of what I saw, imagined, nightmared, or whatever.

But I had moved out of London (*had* to move away from Barrows Hill and memories of Barmy Bill) to Newcastle in the northeast. There was a fairground, which I'm sure was real enough, a scruffy little girl with a yappy little dog, a troupe of really strange people from the Freak House marquee, and finally—as if emerging from nowhere, or from the darkness beyond the fairground's perimeter—there was the Clown on Stilts.

But that's enough, I won't go into it except to say that it ended quite horribly, with that little girl out in the midnight fields, running like a wild thing, and calling…calling—

—Calling in a panic for her suddenly vanished dog: "Woofy! Woofy!"

And I'm sure I remember thinking through my alcoholic haze, *You won't find Woofy, you snotty little girl. I don't think you're* ever *going to find Woofy!*

Later there was evidence of sorts—evidence of a monstrous incursion and a dreadful abduction—but no, I won't go there. As in the case of my first nonesuch, I have said enough…

As for this latest thing, lightning strike Number Three, as I'm inclined to call it: this time I'll try to tell it all; catharsis and what have you. But I have to admit that I was once more under the influence, this time for the last time—definitely. Oh yes, for I've been stone cold sober ever since, which is how I intend to stay despite that I feel justified in saying I have been sorely tempted. But for all that I was intoxicated at the time, still it's barely possible I *might* have been dreaming…no, let's make that nightmaring.

I should start at the beginning:

Just as lightning strike Number One had prompted me to move out of London, so after my experience at the fairground in Newcastle I once again felt the need to change my address: in fact to depart *urgently* from the north-east in its entirety. I would head south again—but *not* the south-east or anywhere close to the capital.

I had been doing fairly well as a reporter with a newspaper in Newcastle and still fancied myself a journalist. Fortunately there was an opening with a small regional newspaper in Exeter. I applied for the job, got it, and moved into cheap, reasonably comfortable lodgings. All went well; inside twelve months I was settled in; I accepted the more or less menial or general work that at first I was required to perform around the office, and despite my newcomer status my co-workers accepted and appeared to like me.

Summer came around and apart from the city itself I hadn't yet found time to explore the region. In fact in all my twenty-nine years on this planet I had never before visited the south-west; Devon and Cornwall were completely unknown territories to me. But now, settled in my new job, and having purchased a five-year-old set of wheels with the proceeds of a small win on the national lottery—a win which seemed to confirm the fact that my luck was finally changing—I decided to have a look around the local countryside, in particular the dramatic Cornish coastline, and took a week out of my annual fortnight's allowance. I would try for the other week later in the year, probably around Christmas or possibly New Year.

The weather was disappointing; Land's End was drab, and the moors more so. Unseasonably cold and blustery winds blew in off the sea, and even a locale as legendary as Tintagel, perched on its storm-weathered cliffs, looked uninviting, with much of its antique mystery lost to a dank, swirling mist.

Feeling let down, a little depressed, I drove south across country towards Torbay, and the closer I got to the south coast the more the weather seemed to be improving. So much so that by the time I found myself on the approach road to…well, maybe the name of the town doesn't matter. And for a fact, I wouldn't want anyone of an enquiring mind to go exploring there, perhaps seeking the location of lightning strike Number Three. No, that might not be entirely advisable.

And so we get to it…and so *I* got to it:

To the small hotel on a hill looking down on the promenade; where, beyond a sturdy, red stone sea wall, the English Channel glinted azure blue in the warm summer sunlight. The tide was on its way in, sending slow-rolling wavelets that were little more than ripples to break gently on the sandy shore. Blankets, windbreaks and parasols were plentiful above the tidemark; below it some dozens of children braved the shallow water, and a handful of adults with trousers rolled up, or skirts held high, paddled at the very rim of the sea, occasionally stooping to gather seashells.

The scene was peaceful, idyllic, irresistible: I could look at it for hours! And, since several of this small hotel's rooms had canopied balconies facing the sea, I could probably do just that. A simple sign inside the lobby's glass doors said "vacancies: rooms available," which helped me make up my mind. It was high season; many of the hotels were full to brimming; I considered myself fortunate to have discovered this quaint old Victorian place.

Leaving the road and following a sign to the parking lot, I drove carefully down a steep driveway to the rear of this once-handsome, now slightly careworn four-storey building, and there found a small, walled rock garden and swimming pool. Below this vantage point, the tiled roofs of a handful of other establishments—hotels and cafeterias—flanked the road down the hillside to the seafront. Parking my car, I stood admiring the view for a few moments more, then used the hotel's rear entrance and climbed two flights of stairs to the reception area…

THERE WERE TWO people at the desk: the receptionist, a pleasant German woman in her late twenties, who I later discovered to be the hotel's general dogsbody, and a pale middle-aged woman, the proprietress, who seemed somewhat nervous and quietly preoccupied. I can't better describe this first, lasting impression she made on me—with her periods of fitful, apparently involuntary blinking, and the way her hands were wont to flutter like caged birds—except to say she appeared more than a little neurotic. I didn't notice this immediately, however, for at first it was the German girl who saw to my requirements.

I asked about a room, if possible one with a balcony facing the sea. She checked in a ledger, ran her finger down the page, paused at a certain blank space and frowned. Then with a brief, obligatory smile for me, she turned a curious, enquiring glance on the pale owner of the place. And:

"Room number, er, seven?" she said. But with the inflection or emphasis that she placed on "seven," it was almost as if she had said "thirteen."

And it was then that I noticed the other woman's agitation. Ah! *That's* the word I was looking for, missing from my previous brief description: her "agitation," yes! A sort of physical and (however suppressed) mental disquiet. She opened her mouth, and her throat bobbed as if she swallowed, but no word was uttered, just a small dry cough.

I turned back to the German girl. "Room seven? Does it look out across the Channel? Does it have a balcony? I'll be needing it for four or five days."

"It is—" the girl began to answer, at which the pale woman found her suddenly urgent voice:

"Seven is a corner room. It only looks half-way out to sea. That is, the view isn't direct. We usually leave it…we *keep* number seven empty, as a storeroom." And nodding—blinking and fluttering her hands—she repeated herself: "Yes, we use it as a storeroom…Well, usually."

Now disappointed and perhaps a little annoyed, I said, "The sign at the main entrance says you have vacancies. That's why I stopped here. So are you now telling me I'm wasting my time? Or rather that *you* are wasting it, by causing me to stop for nothing?"

"Mister, er…?" She managed to control her blinking.

"Smith," I told her. "George Smith." (Actually, that isn't the name I gave her; George might be correct but Smith definitely isn't. I think I'll keep my real name to myself if only for fear of ridicule. And anyway, what's in a name?)

"Well, I'm Mrs. Anderson—Janet Anderson—and this is my hotel," she replied. "And I must apologize, but we've been very busy and I'm really not sure that room seven is ready for occupancy. It may well be full of linens and...and blankets?" She seemed almost to expect me to answer some unspoken question, or perhaps to accept what she'd told me.

"It *may* be?" Frowning, looking from one to the other of the pair, I shook my head. "So what's the problem? I mean, can't we simply send someone to check it out?"

By now Mrs. Anderson's hands (and incidentally, that wasn't *her* name) looked ready to fly off her wrists! "A problem?" she repeated me, and then: "Send someone to...to check it out?"

"Ah...!" the German girl's sigh was perfectly audible, and probably deliberately so. *"Das ist mein fehler! Ich bin schuldig!"* she muttered. And then, reverting to English as she turned to the older woman: "No, no, Madame! I am sorry, but this is my fault. I did not think it was important to tell you that I have tidied and made clean number seven. The room has been empty for quite some time, yes, but is now ready for a guest... er, with your permission?"

Gripping the edge of the desk—in order to steady herself, I supposed—Mrs. Anderson said, "Do you think so? Ready for a guest?" She sounded anxious. "Is it all right? Is it really?"

"I am sure of it." The German girl nodded. "Shall I let Mr., er, Smith see the room for himself? Perhaps he will not want it after all."

She turned and reached for a key in an open cabinet on the wall behind the desk; at which the older woman at once appeared galvanised and quickly moved to block her access. For a moment the scene was frozen, the two women staring hard at each other, until finally Mrs. Anderson gave way and, however reluctantly, stepped aside. Then, blinking her eyes ever more rapidly, in a veritable torrent of words, she said, "Yes of course…by all means…do show him the room…there's no problem…none at all! Be so good as to attend to it, will you, Hannah?"

With which she hurried out from behind the desk, offered me an almost apologetic, twitching half-smile, and without further pause went off into the hotel's cool interior.

More than a little bemused, I could only shake my head as I watched her pass out of sight. It had been a very odd five minutes…

It was as Hannah had said: room number seven was very clean and tidy. Small but spacious enough for me, with its double bed and white-tiled bathroom, it was most privately situated on a split-level landing three steps up from the main floor at that end of the hotel farthest from reception. And I could see why it might be used occasionally as a storeroom: set apart from the rest of the guest-rooms, it could well be that it was originally intended as such, only to be converted at a later date.

Following Hannah through the hotel, which seemed paradoxically empty, I had attempted to orient myself as best possible, only to find it a rambling, irregular sort of place whose design overall was higgledy-piggledy and very confusing. One thing I had noticed for sure: close to the bottom of the three steps that rose to my landing, there was one door that opened into a small bar-room—a little too close for my liking, by reason of my *once*-liking, and I could smell the beer—and another leading to the large dining-room with its panoramic window looking across the bay. To one side there was also a flight of dog-leg stairs marked "Private: Staff Only," that climbed to a landing before angling out of sight toward the front of the hotel. According to Hannah the rooms up there were occupied by a pair of female, casual workers from the Czech Republic—"common room-maids," as she described them, sniffing and tilting her nose—also by Mrs. Anderson, by Hannah herself, and by "the chef."

So much for the interior layout…

As for number seven, the somewhat isolated room I was being offered: "I'll take it," I told her, after opening curtains and double-glazed, floor-to-ceiling sliding doors, and stepping out onto the canopied balcony, from which the view of the promenade and beach was sidelong, less than perfect but acceptable.

"As you wish," Hannah answered, handing me the key. "When you return to reception you may want to check in. Mrs. Anderson insists on payment in advance—by cash or card, whichever you choose, but no cheques—and, if you intend to eat in the hotel this evening, you may wish to order your meal in advance. Now, if there is nothing else, I—"

"Hannah, if you'll permit such familiarity," I cut her off, "may I ask you a rather awkward question?"

"An awkward ques—?" she began to repeat me, then paused to raise a knowing eyebrow before continuing: "Ah! About Mrs. Anderson, I think. Her, er, mannerisms?"

I nodded. "You're very astute."

"No, not really." She shrugged. "Anyone could see that Mrs. Anderson is of a nervous nature. Well, she always has been, but recently..." And there she paused.

"Recently?" I prompted her.

But Hannah shook her head. "No, it is not my place to speak of such things. Not behind her back, and not to a stranger."

"Of course not," I agreed. "It's just that I feel concerned about her. Perhaps I've upset her in some way—something I may have said or done? She didn't seem to want me here!"

Hannah bit her lip, thought it over for a moment, and said, "No, it is not you. It is this place, this area which she finds disturbing..." And looking around the room, and out through the balcony doors, she waved a vague, all inclusive hand at nothing in particular. "Even this room—perhaps especially this room—or some of the things that have happened here."

"Things have happened? In this room?"

She shrugged, stepped closer to the open balcony doors, and looked out. "Out there, and...and up there."

I followed her gaze—out across the ribbon of the road and up a hillside clad in ivy and old man's beard—craning my neck to take in the gaunt aspect of another, rather dilapidated-looking hotel perched up there on that higher level. And:

"Yes," she said, nodding. "Up there,"

"But you also mentioned this room," I pressed her.

"Yes," Hannah said, moving toward the door. "Mrs. Anderson does not like this room. This is the first time she has let it in the eleven months I have worked here. But we had a very poor winter, with only a few guests, and while things are now improving, I know she still needs the money. That is why…" But here she paused.

"Why you argued on my behalf? At the desk, I mean?"

Now she smiled and said, "Aha! But you too are very astute! Also persistent! Myself, I am not a superstitious person. There is nothing wrong with this room Mr. Smith, and I hope you enjoy your stay here."

"But—"

"Now I have work," she said. "You will excuse me?"

While I would like to have known more, what else could I do but let her go?

As she left, Hannah closed the door quietly behind her…

Moving my luggage, a single small suitcase, from my car to room number seven, I stopped at the desk to order dinner and pay for four nights in advance. Hannah was obviously busy elsewhere for when I rang the bell it was Mrs. Anderson who came from a small office at the end of the desk to attend to me.

She looked a lot more settled than the last time I had seen her, and while dealing with the business in hand she was able to talk to me.

"You're from London, Mr. Smith?"

"Ah, my accent!" I said, nodding. "No mistaking London, eh? Well yes, I'm London born and bred, but not just recently. Newcastle, but I wasn't there long enough to pick up the accent—thank goodness!"

She smiled. "I hear lots of accents. I've become expert in recognising them."

"And how about you?" I answered. "I'm no expert myself but I'd guess you're local—or West-Country at least?—or then again, maybe not. It's like I said: I'm no expert!"

"From Cornwall originally," she said. "We owned a hotel in Polperro; that is, my husband and I. But business was very bad three years in a row, so we sold up, moved here six years ago, fell in love with this place and…and bought it."

As she paused her smile gradually faded, then for a moment or two she began that rapid blinking again. She must have seen my reaction however—my startled expression—and as quickly took hold of herself. Then:

"I'm sorry," she began to apologise, "but my nerves aren't up to much these days. I'm sure you've noticed, and…"

I held up a hand to stop her. "There's really no need."

But with her voice trembling ever so slightly, she quickly continued: "…*And* I think that you deserve an explanation. For it might have appeared I was being unnecessarily rude to you."

"Mrs. Anderson," I began, "whatever the problem is, I don't need you to explain. I'm only a little worried that my presence here might be aggravating things…my presence in room number seven, that is."

Despite my apparent concern and words of sympathy, however, my mentioning the room was quite deliberate. Hannah had told me something about that room—she had even made it sound as if it was haunted or something—and I wanted to know more; it was as simple as that. Looking back on it, maybe I should have remembered what people say about cats and curiosity.

Mrs. Anderson seemed to have gone three shades paler. "Room number seven," she finally said. Not a question; nothing emphasized; she had simply repeated me coldly and parrot-fashion…as if my words had triggered some response in her brain causing it to switch off, or at the very least to switch channels. Then the blinking started up again and her hands began fluttering on the desk's mahogany top.

Whatever this recurring condition of hers was, it was obvious that my words had brought on this latest attack. And now my concern was very real.

On impulse I reached across the desk and trapped her hands, pinning them there. She at once relaxed and in that moment, but only for the moment, I almost felt uplifted: some kind of faith healer!…But no, I didn't have the touch; it was little more than concerned, caring human contact.

Sensing the calm come over her, as quickly as I had reacted to her problem I now released her and took a pace back from the desk. And: "I'm…so *sorry*!" I said, not knowing what else to say.

"There's really no need," she answered, no longer blinking and apparently in control once again, but avoiding further eye-to-eye contact by gazing at her slender white hands. "It's not your fault, Mr. Smith. It's a matter of association: that room, and the memories. You see, I loved my husband very much, and—"

She paused, and before she was able to continue—assuming she intended to—the hotel's frosted-glass outer doors beyond the small lobby swung open, and a rising babble reached us as a large party of noisy, chattering people began entering from the pavement in front of the place. Out there, a coach was just now pulling away.

Now Mrs. Anderson looked up, away from me and toward these others as they claimed her attention, smiling and trading small talk with her where they passed us by. And some colour returned to her face when a pair of men carrying a wicker basket between them stopped and nodded, beamed their satisfaction and indicated their burden.

"For tonight," one of the two said with a laugh, "that's if chef will oblige?"

"Oh, I'm sure he will!" Mrs. Anderson answered him. "That's if you'll pay something for his time, Mr. Carson, and if you'll also cover my losses?"

"But of course we'll look after the chef!" Carson answered. "And your takings won't suffer any. These—" he tapped a finger on the basket, "—are only for those who caught 'em, who took a chance and held back from ordering an evening meal. And there's maybe a couple of pounds extra left over for your freezer."

Now she was smiling, albeit a little wanly. "You had a good day, then? You made a good catch?"

"Some nice ling," the other replied. "Wreck-fish, you know? And a few beautiful red mullet! Do you want to see?" He made as if to lift the basket's lid.

"Goodness no!" She turned her face away. "Better get off to the kitchen before you stink the whole place out!"

And laughing, the two made off after the rest of the group.

"A fishing party," I said, unnecessarily; many of them had been carrying their fishing tackle, and they'd certainly seemed overdressed for a warm summer day! Anyway, I now understood why the place had seemed so empty.

"Two coach loads of them," Mrs. Anderson answered. "They've been here for a week, fishing from some boats they've hired out of Brixham. The other coach should be arriving any time now. In a few more days they'll be gone; the place will be mostly empty again and I'll miss their custom. They're no trouble and during the day they're mostly out, but they do use the bar quite a lot in the evenings."

Smiling, I replied, "Where they down a few drinks and start telling tall tales of the ones that got away, right?"

"Myself, I don't really approve of drink," she said, frowning for no apparent reason. "Though I must confess that the bar keeps the place ticking over. Which reminds me: I have stock to take care of. Please excuse me..."

She went off about her business, and as Hannah appeared and began making entries in books behind the desk, once again I was obliged to rein in my curiosity. Then again—as I grudgingly told myself—whatever the mystery was here it wasn't my business anyway. And some ten minutes later, finished with unpacking my few belongings, I was out on my balcony in time to watch the second coach unloading its passengers with their rods and gear. Quieter than the first batch, it appeared that their day hadn't quite matched up to expectations...

I HAD CHECKED into the hotel (which I'll call the Seaview, once again because that wasn't its name) in the middle of the afternoon. Now, with nothing to engage me until dinner, I determined to look more closely at the hotel's exterior, fixing its design and orientation more firmly in my mind.

At the desk I collected a front door "key"—a swipe card—from Hannah, and left the hotel by the front entrance. Outside, I crossed the steeply sloping road's canyon-like cutting to the high-walled far side, where because there was no pavement I was obliged to huddle close to the old stone wall in order to avoid descending cars. And from that somewhat dubious vantage point I scanned the wedge-shaped bulk of the Seaview.

Apart from the canopied entrance, the windows of Mrs. Anderson's office and those of the top floor, which were little more than a row of fanlights—and with one other exception, but an important one—the Seaview's anterior aspect was more or less a blank wall and scarcely interesting, causing me to wonder why I had found the place so attractive in the first place. In just a little while I would discover the answer to that question.

I have mentioned the hotel's wedge shape:

The thick, unadorned end of this wedge was at the Seaview's higher elevation; while the narrow, lower end sported and supported, at a height of some nine feet over the pavement, a lone, canopied balcony: in fact *my* balcony, that of room number seven. And it was because the balcony was set at a skewed angle on the "pointed" or thin end of the building that it was able to offer sidelong views of both the seafront and the hillside...not to mention that other, higher, rather more dilapidated or deserted hotel that loomed up there, set well back from the road in rank and neglected gardens.

Standing in the road's cutting under the massive, backward-leaning retaining wall that was literally securing the hillside, I wasn't actually able to see that place on high; yet somehow I was aware of it, had been aware of it ever since gazing upon it from my room's balcony. Indeed I could sense it—could almost *feel* it—frowning coldly down on the Seaview. Even in the glow of a late summer afternoon I could feel this oppressive weight; or perhaps it was only the fearful tonnage of the hillside that I felt, held back by the great wall...

There in the shade of that wall, just for a moment I felt a chill; or more properly I felt slightly uneasy. But then, as my gaze once more swept the Seaview end to end—and passed beyond the hotel, down the road to the seafront—all such weird imaginings were put aside when I was suddenly reminded what it was that had inspired me to turn off the main road into the hotel's carpark in the first place. Quite simply, it was the view below and beyond the hotel: that of the promenade and inviting golden sands, and the glittering blue waters reaching right across the bay to the horizon. These were the things which had coloured my first impression of the hotel, not the building itself but that marvellous view which it commanded.

As for the intimidating chill I had felt: well, I had been standing in the shade of the great retaining wall, after all…

BACK OVER THE road, I walked along the pavement in front of the Seaview down to the building's "sharp" end under the balcony of room number seven, then turned right to descend the steep drive to the gardens, the pool and parking lot.

By this time the shadows were falling slantingly toward the sea as inland the sun prepared to set behind higher ground. The back of the Seaview, with its double row of canopied balconies, now stood in its own shadow, and looking up at it I finally recognized the extent of my error in perspective. For the *front* of the hotel, with its more or less blank stone wall, was the actual *rear* of the place, while this ocean-facing, far more ornate elevation with its truly wonderful view of the bay was the real front.

The beach was beginning to clear; tourists and other holidaymakers strolled the esplanade where sunlight yet struck home; with two hours yet to dinner, I spent a few minutes watching a lone swimmer performing his expert crawl, to and fro, the full length of the pool, before going in through the Seaview's rear entrance and up to my room…

As if to counter the unseasonal chill which I had felt earlier, the room was very warm. This was, however, in no way unnatural; despite that the hotel's central heating had been shut down for the summer, number seven's floor-to-ceiling sliding glass doors had trapped much of the day's sunlight, and I could still feel its warmth radiating from the walls and floor.

Showering, drying off, and changing for the evening from my rough driving clothes into summer casuals—slacks and a light shirt—I went out onto the balcony. Along with a small table, there was a deckchair which I unfolded and set to a comfortable angle, so that I could sit facing that portion of the bay which my rather awkward sidelong view afforded me.

In a little while, however, becoming aware of the strain on my neck—and sensing once again that indefinable heaviness of atmosphere: an "unparalleled, extraordinary nonesuch sensation" perhaps? Or more properly the feeling that someone's unfriendly eyes were fixed upon me—I repositioned the deckchair to face the road and settled back with my eyes closed, gradually easing the cramps in my neck and shoulder.

More comfortable in that position I began to nod off…only to start awake again as the notion that I was under observation returned in such force that I could no longer ignore it!

Not that there was any way some unknown other could have me under observation…nor any reason he would want to, for that matter! But still I snatched open my eyes, as if to catch someone at it.

Across the road, the retaining wall rose in its own shadow; above it, the steep weed- and ivy-festooned hillside climbed up and back through neglected, overgrown terraces to that frowning scarecrow of a place, the deserted hotel up there. Standing now in early evening shade—with its empty, higher windows behind their balconies staring lifelessly out; also its lower windows, like a row of bleary eyes, gazing over the parapet of a balustraded patio—the place looked more gaunt than ever, and even ghostly.

But that was all. No one was spying on me—except perhaps that forsaken hotel itself, if that were at all possible. Which it wasn't…

…But in any case I narrowed my eyes and studied the place more closely. Not that there was much to study, for the hotel's front was more properly a facade: an Andalusian mask—plaster as opposed to plastic surgery—applied over bricks and mortar presumably in order to enhance the looks of the place, in which task it had failed utterly.

Craning my neck, I stared at the place top to bottom and in that order. Three storeys high, with its close to gothic aspect it reminded me of a desanctified church. Above the flat roof's parapet wall, the hollow, sharply-pointed triangles of ornamental gables were pierced through by shallowly slanting beams of sunlight. Then there was that frowning facade, and finally the patio behind its balustrade wall.

As to the latter:

Because of the steep angle I couldn't see the patio in its entirety, but even so there was something up there that I found just a little odd. While it was obvious that the place had been stripped to the bone and no longer functioned as a hotel, still it appeared that certain of its former embellishments had been left behind.

At each end of the patio and in its centre, standing there like stiff, lonely sentinels, a trio of large, folded-down sunshade parasols continued to watch over places once occupied by hotel guests at alfresco tables. In the case of the parasol on the far right, however, "standing" is probably misleading; for in fact it had toppled and now leaned over the parapet in that corner, where its canvas burden tended to sag a little. At the far left its opposite number remained upright but it, too, had suffered an indignity: its canopy had not been fully collapsed, resulting in bare ribs and a badly torn canvas that flapped in an evening breeze off the sea like a tattered pennant.

Only the central parasol appeared in good functional condition: its stem entirely perpendicular and its folded-down canvas canopy secured at the frill three-quarters of the way down its length. I knew that under that frill eight hardwood spokes would be clasped about the stem in a circle, like the arms of some deep-sea octopus. I understood the design of these things by virtue of the fact that my landlady in Exeter had just such a parasol in her garden, beneath which I would often sit reading a book.

As for this forlorn trio:

Since in their day these sunshades would have been attractive and expensive heavy-duty items of outdoor furniture, I was at first surprised that they had been left behind—especially the pair that appeared to be in good order. That was what I had found a little strange. On reflection, however, I reasoned that just like the parasol with the torn canvas, the other two might also be damaged, their defects hidden or disguised by distance, but sufficient to make salvaging them unprofitable.

Then, as the shadows deepened and my balcony cooled, I went inside, fell asleep on my bed, and woke from disturbing but unremembered dreams barely in time for dinner…

AT DINNER I discovered that the Czech girls—Hannah's "common room-maids"—had duties other than cleaning, tidying and changing the linen: they also served meals. They were pretty girls, too, very much down to earth, unlike the rather haughty Hannah.

"Haughty Hannah"…from Hamburg, or maybe Hannover? I had to smile at the alliterative "sound" of it: even though it only sounded in my mind, it served to bring *back* to mind the title of that novelty song, Hard-Hearted Hannah, about a lady who "pours water on a drowning man." Also, it told me that for some reason I couldn't quite put my finger on I had taken a dislike to the German woman. Perhaps it was because she had "poured water" on my questions about Mrs. Anderson.

Anyway, the Czech girls served dinner to me and a room full of amateur fishermen and women, and the chef—decked out in a white hat and apron—came out of the kitchen to inquire about his culinary offerings: were they up to expectations? And actually they had been; indeed the food had been exceptional.

I told him so in the bar later, where I was drinking Coca-Cola with a slice of lemon, and lusting after his Jack Daniel's Old No. 7 on the rocks. A burly, pigtailed Scotsman—"It keeps mah hair oot o' the grub!"—he appreciated my compliments, and he fully understood why I refrained from joining him in a glass of the hard stuff.

"Oh aye," Gavin McCann quietly announced, nodding and lifting a confidential forefinger to tap the side of his nose. "Mah old man—mah father—he found it somethin' o' a problem, too. He liked his wee dram. Truth is, he liked every wee dram in the whole damn bottle! And he paid for it, the old lad: he saw more than his fair share o' pink elephants, that yin. Until the time came when they stampeded all over him, especially on his liver! Aye, and they made a right mess o' that, too."

Pink elephants? Well, I hadn't come across any of them. But other stuff? Oh yes, I had seen other stuff.

"How about you?" I asked him—and quickly added. "But hey, ignore me if that's a bit too personal! It's just that—"

"Am I an alcoholic, d'ye mean?" He shook his head. "No, not yet. So don't be affeard o' buyin' me a drink or two! Mind you, I've seen enough o' drinkin' in this place—and in the town—not tae mention the Andersons' old place down in Polperro. Aye, and ye'd think it would put a body off; but a man gets a taste, and...well, let's face it: there's no too much else tae enjoy any more, now is there?" With which he tossed back the drink he was working on, stared expectantly at me, and speculatively at his empty glass.

This was rather more than a subtle hint, but with a little luck I may finally have found a means of discovering something more about the Seaview's—or Mrs. Anderson's—mystery, assuming there was such a thing.

And so when McCann was sipping on his next drink, a double I had bought him, and which I wished was mine: "Chef," I asked him, "Gavin, what do you make of Mrs. Anderson, the Seaview's boss lady?"

"Eh?" he answered sharply, narrowing his eyes and lowering his glass. "What's that, ye say? Janet Anderson? Ye've noticed somethin' about that poor lass? Well let me tell ye: she's one very unfortunate lady, aye! But not so unlucky as some I could mention. *Hmm!* Maybe ye'd care tae hear about it?"

I said I would, of course. And as the drink went in so the story came out and the mystery began to unravel; by which time we had moved to a corner table well away from the other guests, where McCann could tell his story in relative privacy...

"UNLUCKY, AYE, JANET and Kevin both," McCann reiterated, with a customary nod and confidential finger tapping his nose. "But as tae who was unluckiest…well, at least Janet's still here!"

"Kevin?" I raised a querying eyebrow.

"He was her husband," McCann answered. "And he had the self-same problem as mah old man and yeresel'—er, no offence! But ye'll ken mah meanin'."

"No offence taken," I answered. "And I'm not convinced that I was ever a full-fledged alcoholic anyway. You see, it affects me very quickly and so badly that I've never been able to drink that much in the first place! But whether or no, I'm off it and glad to be." Which was at least half true: I was off it.

"Enough said," said he, and again his nod of understanding.

"So?" I shrugged, as if only casually interested. "This, er, Kevin is Mrs. Anderson's husband? And he what? Ran off and left her or something?"

He gave me an odd look. "Aye, or somethin'…" But then:

"Ye ken," said McCann, "I've always believed there's only one right and proper way tae tell a story, and that's frae the beginnin'. And for that I'll need tae take ye back tae Polperro all of seven long years ago. That's where they met and wed, and began their first business venture together: a small hotel that was on the slide when they bought it and kept right on slidin'. The Andersons, aye—a *verra* odd couple from the start! Janet, so straight-laced and, well, just straight!—but naturally so, ye ken? I mean: never holier-than-thou, no, not at all. Just a steady, level-headed lass. As for Kevin, her junior by some seven or eight years: he was a wee bit immature, somethin' o' a Jack-the-lad, if ye get mah meanin'. Like chalk and cheese, the pair o' them, but they do say opposites attract. And anyway, who was I tae judge or make observations? Nobody.

"As to who I *really* was:

"I was the top chef on a cruise liner until I lost mah job tae a poncy French cook who was havin' it off with the captain! Anyway, that's a whole other story. The thing is, I was discharged frae mah duties in Plymouth in the summer, and so took time off to rethink mah life. A bit o' tourin' found me in Polperro, and that's where I met up with Kevin in a pub one night. He had a few personal problems, too, for which reason he was sinkin' a dram or two…or perhaps three or four. This was before Janet knew just how dependant he was becomin'—on booze, ye ken.

"But how's this for a coincidence, eh? Kevin and Janet Anderson, they'd purchased their wee place just a month ago, since when a cook they'd taken on had walked out over some petty argument or other. So there they were without a chef, and me, Gavin McCann, I was without mah cook's whites! But no for long.

"Well, I took the job, got mahsel' installed in The Lookout—a place as wee and quaint as ye could imagine, sittin' there on a hill—and cooked mah heart out for the pair; because 'A' they paid a decent wage and 'B' I really liked them. They treated me right and were like family, the Andersons. She was like a little sister, while he…well, I found Kevin much o' a muchness as I mahsel' had been as a young man fifteen years earlier. So I could sort o' watch over her while yet enjoyin' a wee dram with him frae time tae time. That was before his drinkin' got a lot more disruptive; which, lookin' back on it now, didn't take all that long. No, not long at all.

"Ye see, the fact is he couldn't face up tae responsibility o' any kind. Kevin wasn't a waster as such—he wasn't a complete good-for-nothin', ye understand—but simply immature. And when it came tae takin' charge, makin' decisions, well, he just couldn't. Which put a load o' weight on poor Janet's wee shoulders. And him feelin' useless, which I can only suppose he must have, that fuelled the need which only drink could satisfy. And it's a fact that many alcoholics drink because they're unhappy. Kevin was unhappy, I'm certain sure o' that... not with Janet, but with his own weaknesses.

"Now, I've told ye how The Lookout was goin' downhill. That was partly because it had been up for sale, empty for a year or so, and was in need o' repairs, some sprucin' up and a touch o' paint here and there. And bein' located inland a mile or so, it wasn't exactly ye're typical seafront property. Janet's plan—and ye'll note I say *her* plan, because she was the thinker; aye and the doer, too—was tae refurbish the place in the fall and through the winter, when tourism fell off, and get it ready for the spring and summer seasons, when all the grockles—the holidaymakers—would be back in force. O' course, with bills and a mercifully small mortgage tae be paid, it was still necessary that The Lookout should tick over and stay in the black through that first winter.

"Anyway, I ken now that I was perhaps a bit insensitive tae what was happenin' with Kevin; but it was Janet hersel' brought it tae mah attention. She asked me straight out, but in a verra cordial manner, not tae drink so much with Kevin because it was 'interferin'' with business. And I finally saw what she meant.

"Kevin sometimes worked the bar: oh aye, servin' drinks was one of the few things he was good at. In fact he was *verra* good at it! For every drink I bought in the bar when I was done with mah work in the kitchen, there'd be another 'on the house' frae him. And for every free one Kevin served me, he'd serve another tae himsel'. The bar was scarcely makin' a penny because he was drinkin' it up as fast as he took it in!

"But though his eyes might glaze and his speech slur a wee, he was rarely anythin' other than steady as a rock on his feet. That's the kind o' drunk he was, aye. Which I suppose makes his passin' just a might more peculiar. I mean, it was unlike Kevin tae fall, no matter how much he'd put down his neck… But fall he did. Cracked his skull, broke his back, and even crushed his ribs, though how that *last* came about is anybody's guess…!"

When McCann paused to sip at his drink I took the opportunity to get a few questions in. "Kevin's passing? You mean there was as accident: he got drunk, fell and died? My God! But with all those injuries…that must have been some fall, and from one hell of a height!"

"Ye'd think so, would ye no?" McCann cocked his head on one side enquiringly. "But no, not really. No more than nine or ten feet, actually; or maybe thirteen, if ye include the balcony wall."

The balcony wall? And then, as certain of the Seaview's hitherto unexplained curiosities—its mysteries—began slotting themselves uneasily into place, suddenly I saw it coming. But to be absolutely certain:

"And what balcony would that be?" I asked, my own voice and question distant in my ears, as if spoken by some other.

"The one on the corner there," he answered. "The balcony on room number seven, which Janet lets stand empty now, though for no good reason that I can see. A room's a room, is it no? If we were all tae shun rooms or houses where kith and kin died, why, there'd be nowhere left for us tae live! I mean, a body has tae die somewhere, does he no?"

To which, for a moment or two, I could find no answer…

He had obviously seen the look on my face and sensed the change in me. And: "Ah hah!" he gasped. "But…ye came in today, did ye no? And ye found the place full tae brimmin', all except room seven. Well, well! And she actually let ye have it, did she? So then, maybe things are lookin' up after all. And no before time at that."

While I now understood something of what had happened here, there were still several vague areas. Since McCann had intimate knowledge of the Andersons, however—since he'd known them and worked for them all those years—

it seemed more than likely he would be able to fill in the blank spots.

Unfortunately, before I could get anything more out of him, Janet Anderson herself came into the bar-room, smiling and nodding at myself and her chef as she crossed to the bar where one of the Czech girls was serving. The pair spoke briefly over the bar, before Mrs. Anderson headed back our way and paused to have a word with us, or rather with McCann. But:

"Do excuse me," she spoke to me first. And then to McCann: "Gavin, I know you're off-duty and I so dislike disturbing you, but would you mind doing up some sandwiches—say nine or ten rounds—for an evening fishing party? I would have asked you earlier, but they've only just spoken to me. And of course you may keep the proceeds."

McCann was up on his feet at once. "No problem at all, mah bonny," he said. And to me, as he turned to go: "I'm obliged to ye for ye're company—" with a knowing wink and a finger to his nose, "—But now ye must excuse me." With which he was gone…

I TOO HAD stood up at Janet Anderson's approach. Now I offered her a seat and asked if she would like something: a soft drink, perhaps? But she shook her head, saying: "It's kind of you, but there's always work: things to be done, problems to solve." And yet, seeming uncertain of herself and of two minds, she continued to hover there, until finally I felt I had to inquire:

"Is there perhaps, er, something...?"

"Oh, no!" She smiled, her hand on my arm, where I sensed a tremor coming through the sleeve of my light jacket. But in another moment the smile left her face, and taking a deep breath, as if suddenly arriving at a decision, she said, "Please do sit down, Mr. Smith." And as I seated myself she quickly, nervously continued: "You see, I...well, it's just that I've been wondering about...about your room. Room number seven hasn't had a paying guest for quite a while, and empty rooms often develop a sort of neglected, even unfriendly atmosphere. I mean, what I'm trying to say is: do you find the room comfortable enough? Have you any complaints? Does the room feel, well, *right* for you?"

"Why, yes!" I replied. "Everything feels just fine!" Which wasn't exactly true, and I would have preferred to answer: "Why are you asking me such odd questions, Mrs. Anderson? I mean, what *else* is there about that room—other than what I already know of your troubles—that so concerns you?" But since I *did* know at least that much, and since it was obvious that she was close to the edge, I was naturally unwilling to risk pushing her over. And anyway, if anything remained to be discovered, I believed I could probably find out about it later from McCann.

But for the moment, because she was still standing there, I added, "In fact you needn't be at all concerned, because I find the room private and very pleasant. As for complaints: I simply don't have any! I would have to be very fussy to call one small fault a complaint, now wouldn't I? And—"

"—A fault?" she cut me off. "Something...well, not quite right? Something you find just a little, er, odd, perhaps?" Her voice was beginning to shake along with her hands.

"No," I quickly answered, finding her nervousness—or perhaps more properly her anxiety—disconcerting. "Nothing at all that you might call 'odd.'" Which again wasn't the entire truth. "It's just the view, Mrs. Anderson! Just the view from the balcony." By which I meant the partial or sidelong view of the sea-front, the beach, and the blue expanse of the bay itself.

But she obviously thought I meant something else. "The view across the road," she said with a knowing nod. "And up the hill to that awful old place." And even though she was steadier now, still her words had come out as breathless as a whisper.

"No, really—" I began, shaking my head. "I'm only talking about—"

But she had already turned and was moving a little unsteadily away; and over her shoulder, interrupting me before I could continue, she very quietly said, "Well if I were you, Mr. Smith, I wouldn't look at it. Yes, it's best not to look at it, that's all..."

AND THAT DID it. Whatever this thing is in me—this lodestone that forever seeks to point me toward the strange and the nonesuch—I was feeling it now as an almost tangible force. And of course I knew that having begun to investigate I must follow it through and track the mystery down. Because if once again I was about to come face to face with...well whatever, then I damn well wanted to know everything there was to know about it!

And so I stayed there at that corner table, nursing nothing like a real drink, for at least another hour; until it was dark out and the bar had all but emptied; and still Gavin McCann had not returned. Finally, as the last few guests went off to their rooms or wherever, and the Czech girl was shuttering the bar, I went to her and inquired after the Seaview's chef.

"Gavin?" she said, smiling. "Oh, he'll have gone into town. I think there a place where they playing the jazz musics. Gavin like a lot these musics. He going most nights."

More than a little frustrated, I said my thanks, goodnight, and went up to my room. There was always tomorrow...perhaps I could find this jazz bar tomorrow night. But in any case, right now I was feeling tired. It had been a long day.

And a weird one...

I WENT OUT on my balcony, sat in the deckchair in the darkness, with only the street lighting, the glimmer of myriad stars in a clear sky, and the sweeping headlights of vehicles on the steep road for company. Though the flow of the traffic wasn't especially heavy, still the engine sounds of the cars seemed subdued. Which wasn't so strange really, because as I had already noted—and as McCann had pointed out in detailing Kevin Anderson's tragic fall—the balcony was some nine or ten feet above the pavement. This meant that most of the noise was muffled, contained within the road's canyon-like cutting, while the rest of it was deflected upwards by the balcony's wall.

With Anderson's demise in mind, I went to the low wall and looked over. Hard to imagine that someone toppling to the road from here could actually kill himself. Or maybe not, not if he fell on his head. But as for broken ribs: well, that was difficult to picture. Was it possible he'd slipped and fallen with his chest across the wall before he toppled over?

I shook my head, went and sat down again.

The night was refreshingly cool now. To my right, far down below, the glow of seafront illuminations fell on a straggle of couples in holiday finery, strolling arm in arm along the promenade. But I was straining my neck again, and in a little while I averted my gaze, repositioned and reclined my deckchair, and lay back more or less at ease.

Looking across the road and up at a steep angle, I saw the upper reaches of the hillside silhouetted as a solid black mass set against a faint blue nimbus: the glow from the town centre, nestled in a shallow valley lying just beyond the ridge. But as my eyes gradually adjusted, so the silhouette took on a variety of dusky shapes, the most recognizable being that of the derelict hotel.

Where before warm summer sunlight had come slanting through the flat roof's ornamental gables, now there was only the glow of the hidden town's lights…like huge three-cornered eyes, burning faintly in the night. And the longer I looked the more acute my night vision became, so that soon the hotel's entire façade was visible to me, if only in degrees of grey and black shade. But…that feeling, that sensation, of other, perhaps inimical eyes staring at me was back, and it was persistent. I gave myself a shake, told myself to wake up, laughed at my own fancies. But then, when the chuckles had died away, I strained my eyes more yet to penetrate the night, the smoky frontage of that forsaken old place. And as before I examined its façade—or what I could see of it—from top to toe.

First the flat roof and false gables with their background glow: ghostly but lifeless, inert. Next the face of the place: its window eyes—yet more eyes, yes, but glazed and blind—staring sightlessly out over their balconies. And three floors down the balustraded patio with its trio of guardian parasols.

Except now they were no longer a trio, only a pair…

I stared harder yet. On the far right, as before, that one leaned like a bowsprit or a slender figurehead over the corner of the parapet wall. At the far left its opposite number—the one with the partly collapsed canopy—continued to stand upright, but in the still of the night its torn canvas no longer flapped but simply hung there like a dislodged bandage.

So then, maybe the third member of the watch, the one that had seemed intact, had finally fallen over, the victim of gravity or a rotted, broken pole, or both.

But here an odd and fanciful thought. Perhaps there was a *reason*—albeit a hitherto subconscious one—why I imagined and likened these inanimate things to sentinels, guardians, or more properly yet guardian angels: simply that there was something about them. But what? At which point in my introspection, as my gaze continued its semi-automatic descent down the overgrown hillside's night dark terraces, I discovered the missing parasol.

It stood half-way down the terraces facing in my direction. Now I say "facing" because in the darkness it had taken on the looks of a basically human figure that seemed to be gazing out across the bay…or perhaps not. Perhaps it was staring down at me?

Let me explain, because I'm pretty sure that you will know what I mean—that you will have seen and even sheltered from the sun under any number of these eight-foot-tall umbrellas in as many hotel gardens and forecourts home and abroad—and so will recognize the following description and understand what I am trying to say.

At the apex of a parasol, its spokes are hinged on a tough wire ring threaded through a circular wooden block. Now this is a vulnerable junction of moving parts—indeed the most important part of the entire ensemble—for which reason it is protected overhead by a scalloped canvas cowl which also serves to overlap the main canopy, keeping unseasonal rains out. When the parasol is not in use and folded down, however, this cowl often looks like a small tent atop the main body of the thing.

Now, though, with visibility limited by the dark of night, and the canvas canopy not quite fully collapsed, it looked like something else entirely and loaned the contraption this vaguely human shape. The cowl had transformed into a peaked hood, while the partly folded canopy had become a cloak or cassock, so that overall the parasol's appearance was now that of a stylized anthropomorph: it looked "human" but to much the same degree as a snowman looks human. It could be argued, however, that the snowman looks *more nearly* human on account of having eyes—albeit that they're made from lumps of coal.

And as for my having endowed this parasol thing with sight: I think that happened when a motorcyclist coming down the hill rounded a bend higher up, and for a split second his headlight beam lit up the figure on the terrace. Just a split second, in which the shadow under the parasol's hood was briefly dispelled and some bright item or items—in fact two of them—reflected the electric glare of the headlight.

Moreover that same headlight beam continued to sweep, until a moment later it swept me! Momentarily dazzled—as the motorcycle and rider passed beneath my balcony on their descent—I quickly withdrew from whatever reverie or fantasy it was that I had allowed to engulf me. And as my eyes once more adjusted, so the figure halfway down the high terraces was once more a parasol. And nothing more...

While it should come as no surprise, there followed one of the most restless nights I have ever known. I dreamed of unfriendly eyes drilling into me, and the inexorable approach of the floating, pulsating owner of those eyes which I knew—despite that its actual nature remained shrouded and obscure—was nevertheless intent upon harming me. A nightmare, yes, but a persistent one that had me starting awake on more than one occasion.

The last time this happened I got out of bed and closed the balcony's sliding doors, which I had left half open against the warmth of the night. A breeze had come up, causing the curtains to flutter and tap against the glass panes. This must have been the billowing motion I had sensed subconsciously, which my mind had translated into the approach of a fiendish alien power.

So I reasoned to myself, but still it was unsettling…

The next morning following an early breakfast, with the strange events of the previous day and night quickly fading, I set out on foot to go up the hill and down into the valley, exploring the centre of the town; and I came across McCann's jazz bar haunt less than half a mile from the Seaview. It sat out of the way in a cul-de-sac housing various indifferent enterprises—a charity shop, barbershop, hardware store, chemist's shop, etc—and as I arrived it was being slopped out by a fat gentleman in a waistcoat, apron, and rolled-up shirt-sleeves, who went on to sweep up and bin the somewhat more solid debris of last night's entertainment: some bottle glass and pieces of a glass ashtray, empty cigarette packs and cigarette ends, and the flimsy packaging from various fast foods.

Answering my casual enquiry, this fellow told me the place should now be considered closed for a week to ten days: it was being refurbished. Which put paid to any plan I had entertained about finding and questioning McCann here; for the time being I would have to put the mystery of Janet Anderson and room number seven aside. But then again, now that McCann's favourite watering-hole had dried up, as it were, perhaps he would stick more closely to home and the bar at the Seaview. I could always test out this theory tonight.

And I did, but of course that was several hours later. And meanwhile…

…SHORTLY AFTER DINNER, finding the bar empty, I walked downhill to the promenade and turned east along the coast road.

On rounding the point, there, hidden from sight of the Seaview beyond Jurassic cliffs of Devon's unique red rock, I found various amusement arcades, cafes, and fish-n'-chip shops lining the road below the cliffs; and, on the opposite side toward the sea, a modern theatre and a quarter-mile of public flower gardens bordered (astonishingly) by palm trees that flourished here by virtue of Torbay's semi-temperate climate. All very pleasant fare for holidaymakers on the so-called English Riviera, making their all too brief, annual escapes from often drab Midland and northern cities.

But for all that I myself was now a holidaymaker or tourist of sorts, and for all that I should be enjoying the adventure—these new sights and pleasing surroundings, and the soft, salty wafts off the sea—still there was something on my mind. And as I retraced my steps along the seafront my thoughts returned to the parasol as I had seen it last night up on the high terraces; and finally, curiously for the first time, I found myself wondering how it had accomplished its migration from the derelict hotel's patio to its new location.

Well, of course I at once recognized at least one perfectly obvious answer to this riddle: for some reason, someone or ones had moved the thing! But as for what reason that might be...

It was summer, the nights were warm, and there were plenty of young lovers in the town: I had seen and envied lots of them strolling on the promenade. Local folks would certainly know of the deserted hotel, whose empty grounds must surely make an excellent trysting place; and as for the privacy of the neglected terraces and rampant shrubbery...perhaps the shrubbery wasn't the only thing in rampant mode up there!

I'll leave that last to your imagination.

But in any case, that seemed the best answer to the riddle: that some enterprising young lover had moved the parasol to its current location in order to invite his lady-love to a night or nights of passion beneath its sheltering canopy.

And now I know what you're thinking: that I must be a complete and utter idiot, and looking back on it I can't help thinking that perhaps you're right...

Back at the Seaview while I found the bar open, only a handful of the less dedicated fishermen were enjoying a drink. Most of the others were out on a boat in the bay, while a few more had invested in a show at the theatre on the promenade: the "Reanimated Rat Pack Review!" And according to some of the hoardings I had seen during my short walk: "You'll Actually Believe It's *Them*, Direct From 1960s Las Vegas, Alive and Kicking!"

Well "reanimated" or not—dead or alive—I hoped the audience enjoyed the show. But with all the absentees, it did make for a very quiet hotel and bar. And suddenly, out of nowhere, I felt rather alone.

Shortly after settling myself at the same corner table that McCann and I had shared previously, however, who but that self-same Scottish gentleman should appear and proceed direct to the bar. Intent on buying a drink, McCann hadn't as yet noticed me; but as I caught the bar girl's eye and signalled her to put his drink on my tab, he turned and saw me. A moment later he joined me, thanked me warmly for his "wee dram," and without any prompting picked up more or less where our initial conversation had left off:

"So then," he began, "ye're lodged in number seven, are ye? And can I take it all's well with ye? No problems with that wee room? I would have asked ye when last we chanced tae speak, but the dear lady o' the house sort o' interrupted our conversation and I didnae wish tae disturb her by havin' her hear mention o' that room. Aye, and it seems we have similar sensibilities, you and me, for which I'm glad."

"Room seven, yes," I told him. "Which is a very nice room, really! The receptionist, Hannah, appears to think so; but she didn't tell me much about it, didn't go into details. So Kevin Anderson got drunk and died in a fall from my balcony, did he?" I shook my head wonderingly, and continued: "I suppose there's no accounting for the way a tragedy like that—the loss of a loved one—will affect someone. And ever since his accident, Kevin's widow has shunned that room, eh?"

"Hmmm!" McCann pondered, frowning by way of reply. "Shunned it, aye. Well, that's true as far as it goes. Mahsel', I rather fancy she's affeard o' it! It's possible she dwells too much on what happened tae Kevin in that room: the part it played in his…well, while I'm sorry tae be sayin' this, in his frequently drunken deliriums…"

I stared hard at McCann's dour face with its grey, serious eyes. "You were party to the way the room seemed to affect him? As if it had some sort of bad or even evil influence on him?"

"But did I no just say so?" McCann replied sharply, raising an eyebrow. And he sipped thoughtfully at his drink before continuing. "Aye, I was privy tae all such. Oh, I worked for them, it's true, but at the same time I'd become a verra close friend tae both o' them. And I'm still close tae Janet…"

At which point he paused—possibly to consider his loyalty to the Andersons—and I sensed his sudden reticence. I waited, but after several long moments, while I didn't want to seem too eager for knowledge, still I felt obliged to press him; even to bribe him:

"Gavin, let me get you another drink—" I signalled the bar girl, indicating our requirements, "—to wet your whistle while you tell me the rest of it."

"The rest o' it?" he replied. "Well yes, there is a rest o' it—for what it's worth and for all that it's strange—but I must have ye're word on it that it's strictly between the two o' us! We must have respect…not only for the dead but also for the livin', meanin' Janet. Kevin Anderson wasnae a madman, just an addict, a slave tae Demon Drink…" With which he tossed his own drink back, and without so much as a grimace.

Kevin Anderson: a madman? Well it was the first I had heard of that possibility. But:

I nodded and repeated McCann, saying, "As you wish, between the two of us; you have my word on it." But at that very moment our drinks arrived—and both of them were the real thing: two small glasses, full to the brim with amber whisky!

As the girl turned to leave I caught her elbow, explaining, "I didn't want whisky. Whisky for the chef, yes, but I'm drinking Coke—with a slice of lemon!"

"Oh!" Her hand went to her mouth. "I make mistake! I thinking you want same for both! No problem, I take it back." But:

"No need for that!" said the canny Scot, reaching for both glasses. Much to my shame, however, I beat him to it! And:

"What?" he said, seeing me take up one of the glasses. "But ye cannae be serious! Not with ye're problem as ye told it tae me. I'll no be party tae it. Man, with what happened tae Kevin, with what goes on with any alcoholic, I'd have tae hold mahsel' at least partly tae blame!"

"One drink," I told him as the girl moved off. "One and one only. And anyway, surely you can recall my mentioning how I was never a full-blown alcoholic in the first place?"

He nodded. "So ye did, aye. Ah well then, cheers!" And once again he threw back his drink in a single gulp, licked his lips and settled back in his chair. "But no more interruptions, now. Let me get done with it while I'm still in the mood." And after a moment's reflection:

"After we moved in here Kevin's drinkin' really took off. I think maybe he felt even more insecure. That first year, business was only middlin'; they took in enough tae keep their heads above water, but that's all. He was hittin' the stock; she told him tae stop; he began drinkin' in the town. He'd run a message for the hotel—frequently for me, stuff for mah kitchen—and come back two hours later under the influence. It was verra bad o' him, or perhaps not. I mean, it was the booze! He was like a man possessed, and what could he do about it? Oh, it had *such* a grip on him! And yet if ye didnae know him, ye wouldnae ken the state he was in. He kept it hid, drank vodka which is difficult tae smell on a man's breath, managed tae control his speech and balance both; that is, while yet he retained at least a *measure* o' control…

"Aye, but then he took tae sneakin' in, goin' tae room number seven—which at the time was a stock room—and sleepin' it off in there. Janet asked me tae keep an eye on him, tae try and wean him off the drink. *Hah*! Poor woman: she neither understood the insidious power o' the booze, nor the strength o' her husband's addiction.

"Well, I tried: I'd have a drink with him in town, try tae get him out o' there when I thought he'd had enough, then shake mah head and leave him tae get on with it when he'd shrug me off and order, 'just one last drink, Gavin my friend.' For that was the problem: it never was the last one. And that's how it went for three years and more, until a time two summer seasons ago.

"That was when Kevin began tae ramble: his 'hallucinations' and what have ye—which probably had their origin not only in the booze but also in the problems at the old hotel up there on the hill. Aye, that's when the worst o' it began, with all the trouble up there: the weird deaths and what all.

"And it all came taegether as spring turned tae summer…

"First off, a young fellow—fit, full o' life—was found dead in bed in his balcony room, one o' them rooms lookin' down on your room number seven. An autopsy said he'd been smothered, but how when the door was locked from the inside? Accidentally? That didn't seem right at all! His balcony doors were open, but those balconies up there are too far apart for someone tae jump across from one tae the next. So in the end they had tae settle for a respiratory disorder or some such—maybe a heart attack? Asthma? Hay bleddy fever? None o' which quite fitted the bill—and they left it at that. The only other thing: he'd had quite a few drinks, and maybe too many, on the night he died. Accordin' tae the autopsy, however, that hadnae contributed tae what was considered 'death from natural causes.'

"But a mystery? Damn right! And such a mystery that as I've said, I think it may have added tae Kevin's problem, his drunken hallucinations and delirious raving, for after that he got a lot worse. He was forever in that room; he no longer slept with wee Janet at all but we always knew where tae find him: in room number seven, aye. And if he wasnae sleepin' he'd be sittin' on the balcony gazin' out and up at that place on the hill. As for what he saw up there—what attracted him, other than the mystery o' that young man's inexplicable death—well, who can say? But sometimes we'd hear him chunterin' away tae himsel', ravin' on about…well of all things, about a nun!"

A nun? That rang a bell, but one that tolled faintly as yet in the back of my mind. An alarm bell, perhaps? But while I was still trying to locate the source of a suddenly sharpened sensation of unease, McCann was continuing with his story:

"Well, the time came when Janet asked him tae see a psychiatrist: a 'trick cyclist', as Kevin would have it. He must have seen it as a real threat, though, for it did in fact straighten him up…well, for a wee while. But the booze and room number seven—and I think that ghostly place up there—they all had him in their thrall, so that in a matter o' weeks his addiction had the upper hand again and he'd reverted tae his auld habits.

"But ye ken, the locals can tell ye tales about that crumbling place up there; rumour has it that it's always had a verra unfortunate, even a bad reputation. And as tae why I bring that up now: it's because o' another occurrence no more than a month or so after that young fellow pegged it in his room from no apparent cause other than a severe lack o' breath. But actually it was far more than just another incident or 'occurrence': it was the death o' another guest!

"Aye, and would ye believe, it was also another tumble from a balcony!? Indeed the first such tumble, because it took place some weeks in advance o' Kevin's and from a higher balcony. And that's one o' the most irritatin', aggravatin' things about the whole tragedy—Kevin's tragedy, that is: the muchness that the local press made o' it. Ye see, some bleddy journalist ended up theorizin' that Kevin's fall was possibly—even probably—a copycat suicide, o' all unlikely things! What's more, this same so-called 'reporter' must have been doin' some serious snoopin', because he also mentioned Kevin's 'mania', his ravin' and such, which he could only have extracted from one o' the staff here.

"Well o' course Janet sacked the entire gang without delay, except mahsel and Hannah. But too late for poor Kevin, who had already achieved the posthumous reputation o' havin' been a madman…

"Goin' back a wee bit tae the second death up there on the hill: once again this was a young man on his own, and there may have been drink involved. But tae my way o' thinkin': while the booze will put a body tae sleep, it'll rarely find him staggerin' about on a balcony in the wee small hours o' the mornin'!

"Anyway, the experts in the case had their own ideas. Their solution tae this second 'death by misadventure' was that gettin' up tae relieve himsel', this young man had turned the wrong way and, confused by alcohol and still half asleep, had crashed over the balcony wall.

"Now I'm not sayin' that's at all unlikely, ye understand—but I really don't recall too much credence bein' given tae the couple in the room next door, who swore they'd heard him cryin' out and bangin' about before performin' his high dive.

"But anyway that was the end o' that old place on the hill. What with its history, the rumours and all, and two deaths in a row, the place would have been done for even without the people from the Ministry. Oh aye, the Health and Safety men. They came tae check out the balconies—which oddly enough were found tae be perfectly safe!—but as for the rest o' the place: a deathtrap, apparently. And a fire risk tae boot. The owners couldnae sell it so they left it and moved on…

"And that's about it; no more tae tell ye. Except maybe one last thing, which I'm a wee bit reluctant tae repeat because it just might tend tae reinforce that crazy-man theory. Anyway:

"Almost the whole hotel, the Seaview in its entirety, would have heard Kevin's ravin' the night he died. And his last words—words that he shrieked, apparently in some kind o' terror—were these: 'The nun! The nun! Oh Janet—it's the nun!' before the sound o' his skull breakin' and that last long silence.

"It woke me up in mah room all flooded in full golden moonlight, so that at first I thought he wasnae shoutin' about some phantom nun at all. No, he could as easily have been howlin' at the full moon. 'The moon! The moon! Oh Janet—it's the moon!' Except as I've said, that might tend tae corroborate that silly lunatic theory. Or is it really so silly after all?

"*Huh*! Who am I kiddin' if not mahsel'? And havin' hinted as much already, I might as well go whole hog and give ye one last tidbit. Aye, for the moon—that bleddy moon—was a *full* moon on all three o' those fateful, indeed fatal occasions!

"But there, all done and I'll say no more, and ye must make what ye will o' it..."

With which, and without so much as a goodnight, McCann got up and left. And a little while later, so did I. But—

—Just that single shot of whisky had done its dirty work on me, and utterly incapable of resistance I first went to the bar, bought a half-bottle of the filthy stuff, and without even trying to conceal it took it with me up to room number seven...

I REMEMBER SOMETHING of it. Such as sitting on my balcony thinking, drinking. And out there over the night dark sea, a shining silver disc—oh yes, a bright full moon—laying its shimmering pathway on the slumbering waters of the bay.

Lying back in my deckchair and looking the other way, looking up at that great grim shape silhouetted against the glow of the hidden town, my rebellious or simply lying eyes were having more than a little trouble penetrating the darkness on the high hillside terraces. It was the booze, of course, but I persisted...at least until I forgot what I was looking for, only remembering when finally I found it.

Previously it had stood watch up there along with a pair of damaged companion sentinels behind the derelict hotel's balustraded patio wall; then it had reappeared at a location half-way down the terraces, perhaps placed there—or so I had conjectured—by some midnight romeo, to act as a roof over his bower or love nest. And now…

…But, how had it made its way here? To this spot directly across the dark canyon of the road, behind the rim of the great retaining wall, where only its cowl and upper half were visible from my balcony? Perhaps a freakish gust of wind had carried it aloft, tumbling it down the terraces and landing it right-side-up, trapped against the hillside's retaining wall.

Well yes, perhaps. And perhaps not.

But there it was, for all the world like the top half of an eerily human figure—indeed of a cowled nun!—looking down on me. And as a car crested the hill and its headlights shone however briefly on that oddly religious shape behind the high wall, so the darkness under the cowl flashed alive in a pair of triangular flares, which were at once extinguished as the beam swept on.

These things I remember, and also laughing to myself in the stupid way that drunks do, as I stumbled in through the balcony doors to collapse upon my bed…

I FELT IT coming. But don't ask me how; I just knew. Perhaps it was this affinity of mine for weirdness, this magnetism working in my mind, my being. I had felt it, it had felt me. I had seen it, it had seen me. I definitely had *not* wanted to know it, and that could be why I had failed to recognize it: a natural reluctance to engage yet again with the Great and Terrible Unknown. And it very definitely did *not* want its existence revealed!

Of necessity a secretive creature, it had become, unfortunately for me, practised in the erasure of any suspect knowledge of its being. And quite simply—as an adept of this indelicate art—it now intended to erase me!

I felt it coming, its flexible mantle fully open, parachuting on the night air. But immobilized, my mind dulled by drink, I refused to believe; I denied it. It could not be…it was a nightmare…the Demon Drink had filled my mind with monsters. Ah! But what then of the thin people of old London town? Or the clown on stilts as I believed I had once seen him or it? Or had they too been impure and not so simple fantasies of the flowing bowl, mere figments of fermentation, tremens of delirium?

Yet now I could even smell it: a not-quite-taint, a waft of mushroomy fungus spores, a hybrid thing's clammy innards, contracting to engulf and smother me…

My God! I felt it on my face like a slither of wet leather! And knowing that it was real, *I came awake screaming*!

It was there in room number seven with me, inside the wide-open balcony doors, leaning over my bed. Its membraneous canopy was closing over my head, shutting off my air, holding me down. I lashed out with both arms, groped beyond the perimeter of the thing's web. My left hand found and grasped the bedside lamp; I automatically thumbed the switch and dragged the softly glowing lamp inside the living canopy with me.

I was stone-cold sober in a moment, as this alien—what, intelligence?—was illumined from within. And seeing it like that, *literally* from within, I remembered comparing the structure of more orthodox, man-made parasols to the physical form of the octopus. Oh, yes! And now...well it wasn't only the more orthodox ones!

For there beneath its mantle—where, thank God, there was no huge parrot beak but, instead, surrounding a pulsating slit-like mouth, a ring of eight short, worm-like tongues, spatulate at their tips for the delivery of whatever food sustained it—I saw that indeed the thing had tentacular limbs, all eight of them connected by webbing and lined with grasping suckers.

As for the mantle stretched between these limbs: while it was flexible and had the consistency of a bat's wing, allowing my lamp to shine through it, still it had the strength of fine leather and was redolent of the thing's alien essences: anaesthetic odours which were aiding it in my suffocation! Except I wasn't about to die like that, or by allowing it to drag me to the balcony and hurling me over!

Holding my breath, I stopped breathing the thing's poisons and thrust my glowing lamp deep into the ugly gash of its mouth. The lamp, too, had a canopy of sorts: its shade, which crumpled up and fell apart as the electric bulb penetrated the monster's pulsing, dribbling mouth. Only moments ago energized, that bulb couldn't be very warm, but still it was hot enough to alarm the thing.

Muscles inside the mouth closed on the bulb like a ray fish crushing a mollusk—and the bulb exploded with a loud popping sound. The thing's mouth was lacerated internally. It spat thin shards of glass into my face, however harmlessly, thank God; it also spat foul, stinking yellow fluid, its blood, and commenced a violent shuddering as it jerked up and away from my face and upper torso.

Then, trying to yell, I only succeeded in gasping, and when at last I could breathe properly I shouted my outrage. This was as much to hasten the creature's retreat as an expression of my horror. Vivid curses poured out of me as I reached up and tried to throttle its central column, a thin stem of a "body"; and as if these breathy obscenities had helped to inflate it, the monster's canopy bulged and began to open.

Still shuddering, now it convulsed, and chitin hooks on the ends of its flailing tentacles caught on the frame of my single bed, turning it on its side. Saying a silent prayer of thanks, I sprawled on the floor, from where I could see the thing's mushroom shape, its silhouette, against a faint night glow. In full flight now, it was desperately squeezing the bulk of its partly opened canopy out through the sliding doors onto the balcony.

Getting up from the floor I lunged after it. I didn't know what I could do, if anything, but I was more angry than afraid. It wasn't my fault that this creature, like others I had known, was attracted to me—or me to them, whichever—and I wanted it, them, to know we could fight back, that men could be deadly dangerous too.

And still shouting at the top of my voice I rushed out onto the balcony where, fully inflated, the monster was now drifting aloft. How such a thing could fly or glide—well, don't ask me—perhaps by generating gasses within its mantle? I don't know. But anyway I tried to get hold of the clawed, club-like foot at the base of its slimy stem of a body. It was a wasted effort; I couldn't get a grip and those retractable claws were sharp.

In another moment it was gone, rising into darkness, ascending by means of unknown gravity-defying abilities, assisted by the smallest of breezes off the sea.

"Damn you, you bastard thing!" I yelled after it, and suddenly realized that for some little time I'd been hearing a loud hammering at my door. And there I was, leaning across the balcony wall, when the door to the landing crashed inwards from its hinges and Gavin McCann lurched into the room. Close behind the Scotsman came a shrill Janet Anderson, both she and he in night clothes under their dressing-gowns.

While a single dim night-light was burning on the landing, the ceiling light in my room had remained switched off since I came up from the bar. Which meant the eyes of the newcomers—my would-be rescuers—would take a moment or two to adjust to the gloom. And indeed I clearly heard McCann's gasping, urgent question: "Damn! Where's the bleddy light switch?"

That and Janet Anderson's trembling, panted answer: "Here, Gavin—I know where it is—let me do it!" But then, before she could find the switch:

That smell, a faint fungus reek wafting down to me where I leaned out across the balcony wall and scanned the sky. It came from…from over there, yes, borne on the breeze off the sea! And as I turned my eyes toward the bay at that awkward angle, I saw something blot the moon in the instant before the monster's clawed, club-like foot swung at me like a pendulum, catching in my shirt.

I was almost but not quite dragged bodily from the balcony; I felt my shirt rip, and I fell! I fell—

—But on the *inside* of the wall. Brilliant lights flashed in my head as my skull cracked against the top of the wall; my body flopped to the floor; and the very last thing I remember: Janet Anderson's arms cradling me, and her sobbing, hysterical voice fading into a painful, rushing darkness as she questioned me: "What happened, Mr. Smith? What did you see? Was it… was it the nun?"

And then, nothing…

I HAD SUFFERED a cut scalp and very bad concussion, which kept me out of it for four days, three of which I was semiconscious and had my doctors fearing there could even be some brain damage. While that might seem serious enough, poor Janet Anderson had suffered rather more: a total nervous breakdown. She spent a month in what was referred to euphemistically as "a refuge," the secured mental wing of a local hospital.

As for the Seaview's chef, bless his heart: in addition to cooking and helping Hannah to run the hotel, Gavin McCann dedicated what was left of his time during that period to visiting Janet Anderson and myself in equal measure: his employer out of friendship and loyalty, and myself, oddly enough, out of guilt. And it was during one such visit after I returned to full consciousness that he asked me what it was all about: what exactly had I seen?

But I didn't tell him. For from the moment I had opened my eyes to perceive the world afresh, I had been thinking it over. And I had come to a conclusion, settled on an explanation which I might at least *attempt* to believe. For let's face it, I still could not state with absolute conviction that there really were thin, telegraph-pole-tall people in London; I couldn't swear to them any more than to pink elephants! And likewise clowns—or at least one such—on stilts!

What, a clown with stilt legs, and wings? A clown who flew away with a small girl's smaller dog and who would, presumably, if they were available, fly off with other rather more meaningful small things? No, of course I couldn't believe in him. Not while it was even remotely possible that he had been…well, simply a strikingly original clown, and what I had made of him had been fevered guesswork, imagination and hallucination, but mainly nightmares spawned in a bottle of booze.

That is what I told myself to believe; I must at least *try* to believe in that. Because if I failed to do so, then I might have to accept advanced degenerative alcoholic madness. And as for the latter:

Well, Gavin McCann was able—in his way and mistakenly or not—to corroborate something of what I was forcing myself to accept. And seated by my bed wringing his hands, on that occasion when I had nothing to tell him: "I blame mahsel'!" he said. "Me and the bleddy booze both! I should *never* have let ye take that short, not knowin' how it was with ye! Aye, and Janet and me, we found ye're empty bleddy bottle on the balcony. Man, ye must have been drunk out o' ye're mind!"

Well yes, maybe then. But no more…

AND SOMETHING A little over a month later—after reading in my Exeter newspaper about a hotel fire in a certain resort: an unsolved case of arson in a disused, derelict building, according to a police report—I called McCann on the number he'd given me to find out what he knew.

"Aye, that old place on the hill," he told me, guardedly I thought. "I was in the bar and heard the sirens. Janet was out in the town doin' some late shoppin' when it went up. She came in and we watched the blaze taegether. But it was arson, definitely. Why, we could smell the petrol fumes right down there on the balcony o' room number seven!

"And do ye know what? That poor woman's been right as rain ever since!"

SO THERE YOU go. I've told myself I can stay off the booze and avoid further imaginary confrontations, or I can take the occasional drink and suffer the consequences, whatever.

But you know, when my mind is clear and the night is dark, I lie in my bed and turn things over in my head, and then it's as if I am fully in touch with *un*natural Nature. I've heard of the octopuses that imitate coconuts to "stroll" on their dangling tentacles through dangerous shallows. I've read of insects that imitate leaves, and seahorse fishes that are indistinguishable from the seaweeds they live in. There are so many kinds of insects, plants and animals that pretend for their security or, as often as not, their fell purposes to be other than they are. And there are thousands of small species that aren't even catalogued as yet.

And that's only the *small* species…

As for me and my problem, if indeed I have a problem other than the alcohol: can it be coincidence, pure and simple? Or is it that I am in fact a lodestone, a lightning-rod for the weird and the wonderful? Because if the latter is true, then it seems I'm actually destined to be drawn to such things: to these thin people, these clowns-on-stilts, these nuns and nonesuches.

In which case so be it.

But if I can't avoid them, you can at least be sure I'll be looking out for them!